CRUEL OBSESSION

USA *TODAY* BESTSELLING AUTHORS

J.L. BECK & C. HALLMAN

Copyright © 2020 by Bleeding Heart Press

Beck & Hallman LLC

Cover by C. Hallman

All rights reserved.

No part of this book may be reproduced in any form or by any electronic or mechanical means, including information storage and retrieval systems, without written permission from the author, except for the use of brief quotations in a book review.

1

Paranoia skates down my spine as I walk a little bit faster down the sidewalk. The cold night air fills my lungs, and my heartbeat thuds loudly in my ears. All I can see and feel is that creeper from the party coming up to me and grabbing my wrist. His fingers biting into my flesh. The smell of alcohol on his breath as he spoke into my face.

"*Dance with me...*" He didn't ask, he demanded, and there was no way I was going anywhere with him, so I kicked him in the nuts and left the party. But now I can't help but feel like he's following me.

Reaching the end of the sidewalk, I chance looking over my shoulder. My gaze falls on nothing but darkness. The light pole above my head does very little to illuminate the street, and when I look back again before crossing the street, I find someone walking toward me.

Panic bubbles up inside of me, and this time, I start running. The air rips through my hair, and my lungs burn as fear implants itself deep in my gut.

Run. Don't look back. Just keep running.

Cutting down a side street, I hope to throw the guy off, but as I continue running, I can still hear his footfalls behind me. This has to be a nightmare, something I'll wake up from any second now.

Glancing over my shoulder, I realize it's anything but a dream. My eyes catch on the plaid pattern of the man's shirt. Instantly, I know this is the creep from the party. *Shit.* Instinct tells me to run, but deep in my gut, I know what I should do.

My hands shake as I try and pull my phone out to dial 9-1-1, but my fingers slip over the sleek device, and I keep putting the wrong passcode in. Panting, I make it underneath an illuminating streetlamp and force shallow breaths into my lungs.

A grunting sound meets my ears, and when I look over my shoulder again, the man is gone. Just gone, vanished like he wasn't there at all.

Dazed, I stare at the exact spot he was in, fearing he'll reappear any second, but he doesn't. A strange calmness washes over me. It makes zero sense, but I don't dwell on it long enough to digest it. Instead, I shove my phone back into my pocket and run the rest of the way home.

By the time I reach my apartment, the exertion is evident, I'm gasping, and a sheen of sweat has formed against my forehead. I fumble with my keys, almost dropping them before finally getting the damn door open. Once inside, I slam the door closed and lock it before turning and sagging against the door.

A moment later, Max is by my side. The eleven-year-old cat I rescued from being euthanized last year has been my most trusted friend. I sink my fingers into his long fur and let his low purring calm me.

You're okay, everything is okay... I repeat to myself.

It's been years since I'd felt fear like that, not since I was a little girl living in foster care. My skin crawls, and I suppress the thought.

All that matters is that I'm safe. That I'm in my apartment and nothing happened to me.

Everything is going to be okay...

2

S lamming my fist into the fucker's face, I watch with glee as agony overtakes his features. He should've known he would die, especially after touching what was mine.

An image of *my* beautiful Dove fighting to get away from him. Her big, blue eyes brimmed with fear, her plump bottom lip trembling. Clenching my fist, I let the anger from that memory sink deep into my bones.

"What were you planning to do when you got her alone? Huh? Why were you following her?" I growl, my patience withering away with every passing second. Part of me doesn't want to know what he had planned, but the other, bigger part does. I want to hear the words, want them to fuel my anger even more.

"I don't know what the fuck you're talking about," the bastard sneers, playing stupid.

I cock my head to the side and give him a bemused expression. "You must think I'm a fucking idiot, huh? That I didn't see her tell you no. That she didn't push you away? Or that I didn't watch her run out of the house and down the street? That I didn't see you follow a short while later."

If it wasn't for me, he would've hurt her, but I *was* there, just as I've always been. And just like all the others who have tried to hurt Dove, he too will die at my hands.

"You're fucking crazy!" he spits. Blood drips down his lip from the punch I landed against it, and all I can do is stare at it. I can't stop the cruel smile that splits across my face. My blood sings with joy, and the dark beast inside me cheers with elation at the sight of his blood.

Grabbing him by the hair, I tip his head back, reveling in the scream that pierces the air. *Ahhh, there is nothing like when they scream or beg for me to let them go.* The hope that shows in their faces before all is lost. Before I snuff the light out of their eyes with my hands.

"Crazy? You haven't seen anything yet," I sneer.

Clenching my fist a little tighter, I pull back my arm and land another punch, this time, my knuckles meet the bridge of his nose and the satisfying crunch of bone cracking fills my ears.

The monster inside me is terrifying, real, and it consumes me. I don't stop as his screams continue to echo through the warehouse. They all cry and beg, but at the end of the day, it's their own fault. Had they made a better choice, they wouldn't be here.

By the time I'm done, his face is unrecognizable, and he's slumped over in the chair I've tied him to. Turning, I grab a knife and lift his chin, or what's left of it. Then I slice him from ear to ear. I feel nothing as I do this, no that's not true. I feel something. Joy, happiness, relief. His death makes the weight on my chest a little lighter.

Dove is safer now that I've extinguished him. Safer now that another worthless person is gone from her life. Another person wanting to hurt her that won't ever get the chance.

I was put on this Earth to protect her, to ensure her safety as long as I lived.

I might never have her in the way I want, but at least I can always make certain no one hurts her. She will forever be mine, even if she doesn't know it.

Walking away from the body, I head to the sink and wash the blood from my hands. I spend way too long watching the reddened water swirl down the drain. When it finally runs clear, I scrub my hands with soap, rinse, and dry them. Pulling out my cell, I text Rob to tell him to get the cleanup crew together.

Most people would probably feel guilt or at least some type of emotion after doing what I just did, but I don't feel anything.

Not that I can't feel at all, because I can, I just chose not to. Feeling all the time would make it hard for me to kill people for the mob, on top of protecting Dove.

My phone chimes and I see Rob's name flash across the screen, letting me know that he's gotten my message. When he arrives, I walk out to my car like nothing ever happened. I consider just driving home, but at the last second turn onto the street to Dove's place.

She lives in a relatively safe area, but that didn't stop me from putting cameras and motion sensors in her house. I would go to any length to ensure her complete safety. Even in the safest neighborhood in the country, no one knows what happens behind closed doors.

Parking on the street a few houses down, I shut the car off, and look up at the apartment building. *How much longer can I do this?*

Subject myself to her sweet scent, soft murmurs, and beautiful face. How much longer can I go on before I'm forced to claim her? My need for her is starting to consume me, eating away at every single rational thought that I have. Every day I'm forced to tamp it down, but I'm not a saint, and soon enough, I'll break.

Forcing the thoughts away before they take root, I exit the car and walk across the street at a leisurely pace. It's quiet, and if you look hard enough, you might see a few stars hanging in the night sky. When I reach the door to the apartment building, I slide my keycard into the door, waiting for the click to push it open. No one even glances my way as I walk inside. I've been here so many times most people probably think I live here.

In fact, I know one of Dove's neighbors actually thinks I do. Of course, I don't correct her. What would be the fun in that? I use the walk upstairs to clear my mind, and by the time I reach Dove's door, I'm a little more composed. Pulling out my phone, I check the surveillance feed in her bedroom one last time. The image confirms that she's sound asleep, tucked nicely into her bed. Unlocking her door, I enter her apartment slowly. I've done this so many times it's like riding a bike to me.

Quietly, I close the door behind me. I'm welcomed by the darkness of the apartment, feeling at home in more than one way. The dark is where I thrive and the shadows my best friend. It's the only place I can be myself. But Dove, she is light, pure, vibrant, and innocent. My darkness threatens to taint that light, to snuff it out... and that reminder alone keeps me away, but never too far.

I've only taken one small step inside, but Max is right there, curling his fury body around my leg, purring loud enough to wake the dead. He, too, thinks I live here. Bending down, I pat the top of his head before shushing him away.

The soles of my shoes make little noise as I move through the house like a ghost. I know where every corner, every creak, and every piece of furniture is. I know about every window and every door, and even what's hidden in each cupboard. I know how she likes her coffee, what her favorite books are, and what time she gets up every morning.

There isn't one thing about Dove that I don't know about. I know her inside and out, maybe even better than I know myself.

Standing just outside her half-open door, I clench my jaw. Her sweet scent of vanilla and sugar surrounds me. The scent stirs a deep primal need within me. One that urges me to go to her and claim her completely, without mercy or care. It slams into me, gripping me by the balls and urging me forward. I don't want her to be mine. I need her to be mine.

Swallowing thickly, I grapple for control. The beast wanting to be set free so he can mark her. Barely containing myself, I sneak into the bedroom. There's a tightening in my stomach when I first see her. It's like butterflies taking flight, like riding a roller coaster. She's lying partly on her stomach, her cheek resting against the sheets.

Dark brown locks of hair shield most of her face, and I'm forced to suppress a laugh, realizing she's kicked most of her blanket to the edge of the bed. Parts of her are still the same, while others have changed. Drinking in the view before me, I become mesmerized by her perfect legs that lead up to a plump ass. Her firm globes are covered by a pair of sleep shorts that leave very little to the imagination. Saliva fills my mouth at the thought of parting those thighs and licking her virgin pussy, feasting on it, eating until I've had my fill.

Fuck, I wonder what she would taste like; if she would beg me to stop or beg me to keep going? My muscles clench, and my cock presses against the zipper of my jeans painfully. It'd be so easy to take her right now, to cover her mouth and take what I want, to sink deep inside of her and let her innocence coat my cock... Taking a step toward the bed, I almost give in to the urge, but at the last second, I pause and curl my hands into fists to stop myself from touching her.

One taste would never be enough. I could never give her up, so I'll refuse myself while I still have the strength. Letting my gaze wander, I move to her heart-shaped face. Long lashes fanning out like crescent moons against high cheeks. Soft, pink lips that are slightly parted, and an adorable button nose. *My angel.*

I don't know how long I stand staring at her, watching as her forehead wrinkles, and she rolls over, tossing her leg over a pillow.

Every inch of me is being pulled toward her, and when I can't withstand the burn any longer, when the pain in my chest becomes too much, I pick up the blanket and cover her back up. She murmurs something inaudible in her sleep, and I force myself to walk away even when everything inside me is screaming to go back there.

This is something I put myself through almost every night. Loving Dove is my greatest weakness, but I won't give it up... I can't. No matter what I do, no matter how many people I kill, she will always be mine. The devil already owns too much of my soul for me to allow myself to let her go.

The love I have for her is the only good thing left in my life, the only thing pure, and that's why I won't ever take from her. I won't ever hurt her because if I ever do, then there would be no light left in me, and the darkness would swallow me whole.

Without a sound, I leave her apartment and walk back out to my car. Each step is heavier than the last. *When will I stop putting us both through this pain? Never.*

Maybe I would have an easier life if she wasn't in it. If I would just let her go and stop watching her. But I will never stop because Dove deserves a happy life. She needs to be safe, and someone needs to protect her from the monster who lurks in the dark.

And who is better to protect her from them than one of them?

3

No matter what I do. I can't shake the strange feeling that I'm being watched, it's been like this for years. Going to the grocery store, on the drive to work, even in my apartment. It always feels like there are eyes on me, but every time I look up, there's nothing there. No one is watching, at least not that I can see. I do my best to brush off the feelings, but it's a lot harder than you'd think.

I'm pretty sure no one is actually watching me. I mean, why would someone do that? I'm no one. It makes more sense that I've imagined all of this, especially after the incident with the creeper the other night.

This is my body's way of staying guarded after having a shitty childhood. At least that's what the therapist tells me. I keep thinking about stopping seeing her because I'm tired of being reminded of the past. I don't care to remember my time in foster care, and I honestly don't understand why I keep finding myself going to the appointments.

Stopping by my favorite coffee place on the corner, I order an iced coffee hoping the caffeine will make me feel better. By the time I get to the shelter, I've downed the large cup and feel no better. Except now, my bladder is screaming at me. I rush inside, heading straight for the bathroom.

Stupid coffee.

"Good morning," Sasha greets me as I rush past her.

"Morning," I call as I slip into the bathroom. Sighing, I empty my bladder and vow never to drink that much coffee that fast again. When I'm done, I wash my hands and walk back out into the receptionist area.

"Too much coffee?" Sasha giggles.

"You know it," I admit. "I don't know when I will ever learn." I shake my head.

"We got two new surrenders this morning. One of them is a puppy," Sasha tells me. "They only had the dog for three weeks, then realized they would have to actually spend time training the dog not to pee and poop in the house."

"Ugh, why do people get dogs if they can't take care of them? At least the puppy will be easy to adopt out."

Making my first round through the shelter, I make sure all the animals have water and that their cages are clean. There isn't much I can do for all these poor creatures, but at least I can make sure they're taken care of while they're here. Make sure they're fed, warm, and get some human interaction.

Stopping at the last cage that holds the new puppy, I smile. It's some kind of shepherd mix, but its breed doesn't matter, not when it's as cute as it is.

"Yeah, you definitely won't last long, not with that face." The pup is looking at me with big, brown eyes and a wagging tail. It isn't unusual for me to talk to the animals. I don't feel bad or weird about it. Not when the truth is, I'd rather talk to them than to another human.

"Did you see him?" Sasha coo's when I head back to my desk.

Withholding an eye roll, I nod. "Yes, I saw him, and no, you cannot take him home with you. Henry would shit bricks if you brought another dog home."

Her lip curls into a frown. "Maybe I should get rid of him then? The dogs never let me down." This is an ongoing thing with Sasha, she loves Henry, and he loves her, but they're always fighting about something.

"Tell me, are you on or off again?"

"Neither."

"Right..." I shake my head.

"What about you? You find anyone to share that huge apartment with yet?" I shoot her a look that says, *really?*

"I don't date, Sasha. You know this."

"Sorry, I thought maybe you met someone the other night, and that's why you left so early. I didn't even get to ask you what happened?"

Goosebumps pebble my flesh at the reminder. "Yeah, about that, I, uhh... I left because there was this guy that wouldn't leave me alone. He followed me when I left, and then right before I was going to call 9-1-1, he disappeared."

Sasha stares at me wide-eyed. "Holy shit, are you okay? Why didn't you call me and tell me what happened?"

Truthfully, calling Sasha wasn't even something I'd think to do. All my life, I've been alone. I didn't know how to rely on someone else because it had only ever been me.

"I don't know. I just... I was thankful that I had gotten away. I'm really lucky... it could've been much worse."

The thought of being raped and beaten, and then left in a gutter somewhere makes my stomach churn. You hear about it all the time in this city, but no one ever thinks it will happen to them, not until it does.

"Not to sound like a total bitch because I do care about you and would never want anything to happen to you, but you're the luckiest person I know. I mean, the guy just disappears? That never happens, and now that I'm thinking about it, you seem to be lucky all the time."

My brow furrows in confusion. "What do you mean? I'm not lucky."

Sasha gives me a disbelieving look. "Really? You don't actually believe that, do you?" When I don't say anything, she continues, "Let's take your apartment, for example. It's in one of the safest, nicest areas of the city. The rent there is insanely low, and the waitlist for that place is like a mile long. Yet, you somehow got in, and on top of that, you got a discounted rate on your rent."

"Yeah, I still don't know how that happened either." I truly don't. All I did was submit an application and hope for the best.

"What about how you got your car? The guy just wanted it gone so badly, he gave it to you for a fraction of the cost? Then, after all of that, even brought it to you because you didn't have a way to get over there. Come on, you've got to see it too?"

"I mean, I see it, but I don't know if I would consider it luck."

Sasha rolls her eyes. "Girl, start playing the lottery because you're a good luck charm."

All I can do is shake my head and laugh at her. I'm not lucky, not really, right? As we work throughout the day, answering calls and setting the animals up to find their forever homes, I can't shake the conversation away and come to the conclusion that I truly am lucky.

I escaped death the other night, or at least something that would've been close to it. I went to college and got a nice place to live, and a car for a really good price. This job even fell into my lap, so I suppose I agree with Sasha a little, though I won't tell her that.

It'll go straight to her blonde head.

Doing our final walkthrough, I stop at the new puppy's cage. "Don't worry, buddy, you won't be here for long."

"Who are you talking to?" A voice startles me, and I jump back half a foot and grip onto my chest, my heart beating right out of it. Looking to the side, I see Shawn standing only a few feet from me.

"Jesus, Shawn, you scared me," I say, the words coming out in a rush as I try and calm myself.

Giving me a dimpled grin, he says, "Sorry, didn't mean to use my ninja skills on you."

"Next time you scare me like that, I might need to use *my* ninja skills on you. Which consists of a punch in the face." I say, smiling.

"Whoa." He puts up his hands, showing me his palms in surrender. "Easy killer. I'll try not to sneak up on you anymore."

"You better, for your own safety," I joke. Shawn has been working here for a few weeks now, and we've quickly become friends. We joke and laugh together all the time, which are two things I always welcome. Plus, it helps that he's good looking, not that I spend my day checking him out or anything. It's hard to ignore his dreamy, blue eyes, and model-like features.

"So... I was actually wondering what you're doing tonight?" he asks as we are walking back to the front.

"Tonight? Ahh..." I look at him wide-eyed. Is he trying to ask me out? "Nothing, I guess," I finally say.

"Cool, I was wondering if you wanted to grab something to eat... with me?"

"Yes," I blurt out before thinking about it. *Way to sound desperate, Dove.*

Shawn chuckles. "Okay, I guess that's a yes. Do you just want to meet there, or I can swing by your place, and we can go together?" He shoves his hands into the front pockets of his jeans. I should probably meet him somewhere, but I've always dreamt of going on a real date where the guy comes to the house and picks you up, so I push the paranoia away. Plus, it's been forever since I went on a date or was asked out on one.

I smile up at him, my belly filling with butterflies. "Yeah, that would be great."

"I'll pick you up at six. Send me a text with your address." We pause in the foyer, and when he smiles at me, my heart skips a beat.

"Uh, yeah…" I stutter. Jesus, I need to work on my skills. Shawn waves goodbye to Sasha and then winks at me before walking out. As soon as he's out of earshot, Sasha pounces.

"Oh, my god, he finally asked you out. Jesus, I never thought that was going to happen. The boy has been watching you since he started."

My cheeks start to warm. "He has not!"

Sasha nods. "Yup, and now you've gone and made his dreams come true."

"It's just a date, not like we're getting married or anything."

"*Yet*… not getting married yet."

Ignoring her, I get my stuff together and prepare for my drive home. I can't believe I have a date. A real date. Not that I'd have a fake date or something, or that I'm so ugly that no one finds me attractive, but it isn't often that guys ask me on dates. Usually, I find I have to build up the courage to do it.

"I'm so proud of you, Dove. Maybe tonight will be the night." Sasha wiggles her eyebrows.

"Shut up," I say, laughing as I get into my car.

AFTER SPENDING an hour curling my hair, I move on to my makeup. I don't wear it often, mostly due to my lack of skill when it comes to putting it on. Taking my time, I apply the foundation, add some eye shadow, and only manage to stab myself twice in the eye with the mascara. After, I walk into the bedroom and start pulling every dress I own from the closet.

Yes, I know it's just a date, and we see each other every day at work, but I want Shawn to see me as more than the girl in always sees in jeans and a T-shirt. I want him to maybe wonder what's underneath. Shaking my head at the thought, I find a cute dress and decide to pair it with some dark tights and heels.

For a moment, I stand in front of the mirror in my bra and panties, trying not to look at my reflection, but like a magnet, my eyes are drawn to it. It's like the sun, you know it will hurt your eyes, but you still want to look at it.

As soon as I see myself in the mirror, my eyes find the ugly scar marring my otherwise smooth stomach. My hand raises on its own to touch the raised skin. It's an old habit I can't seem to shake. Running my fingers over that horrendous scar, I try not to let the memories of how I got it bubble up.

Instead, I worry about what Shawn might think if he gets a chance to see it. Will he think I'm disgusting? Will he ask questions? Would I be able to answer? Pushing all of those concerns aside, I grab the dress and start slipping into it.

Once dressed, I smooth my hands down the front of the dress and look at myself in the mirror.

I can't help but smile at how well put together I look. Applying a thin layer of gloss to my lips, I give myself the once over one last time and then make a beeline to the kitchen for my phone, purse, and a light jacket.

Checking the time, I bubble over with excitement, realizing he should be here soon. Sitting on the couch, I wait like a child on Christmas morning. Max greets me with a purr as he brushes against my leg, begging for attention as he always does.

Scratching the top of his head, I look down at him. "I can't believe it, Max. I've got a date." I'd hate to be that crazy cat lady who sits at home and talks to her cats, but if I don't get a roll on this whole dating train, that's the path I'm headed down.

Anxiously, I watch the clock, and my excitement slowly turns to disappointment as the minutes continue to tick by without any sign of Shawn.

Opening my text messages, I check to make sure I gave him the right address, which I did. I contemplate sending him a message, and after going back and forth over it, I decide to keep it simple and just ask if he's still coming. Maybe he had something come up? Maybe he can't figure out where I live? I try and come up with any excuse I can, but deep down, I know it's not really any of those things.

It's pitiful how long I stare at my phone, waiting for a text message to come through that never does. An ache forms in my chest after a short time, and stupidly, tears fill my eyes and slide down my cheeks. I swipe at the treacherous tears, wishing I didn't care so much.

There must be something wrong with me. I know I'm not that pretty, but I don't think I'm worthy of always being left in the cold. Every time I have a date, they either don't show, or there is never a second one even though the first goes great.

Swallowing down the pity I'm feeling, I change out of the dress and into an oversized T-shirt and then go into the bathroom and wash my face. It's obvious, he's not coming, and even more obvious, he doesn't plan to apologize for standing me up.

When I'm done, I crawl into my bed and pull the covers over my head.

What is wrong with me? Am I that repulsive? I don't want to think about it, but maybe I'm not meant to be with anyone. Maybe I'll actually become the cat lady with thirty cats, and her virginity intact. God, I hope not, but what are my other options? I can't find a guy who wants me if I can't get him to ever go on a second date, let alone a first.

After a while, I doze off, hoping tomorrow will be a better day.

4

Her tears kill me more than anything. I'm a bastard for doing this to her, but I can't help it. The thought of seeing her with another guy is unbearable. It's easier to make the guy disappear than let her think she'll ever have a future with him.

The organ in my chest tightens as I watch her crawl into bed on my cell phone screen. I wish I could wipe her tears away. Tell her that everything is going to be okay. That she has me forever and doesn't need anyone else.

I doubt she would welcome me with open arms into her life. If she knew the things I'd done, and continue to do, how obsessed with her I am... how closely I watch her, and how often I'm inside her house, she'd be terrified, and I never want to see her look at me with fear in her eyes.

Shoving my phone back into my pocket, I look out at the bright neon sign that's flashing back at me. I had just finished with the Shawn guy when Christian called me for a job. He asked me to swing by Venus, the mob's strip club.

Upstairs is the strip club, but downstairs they maintain a brothel. Everyone in this town is paid off, the cops, the judges, any one of importance is paid blood money to keep their mouth shut because when you fuck with the wrong people, they send me to take care of you.

Forcing myself out of the car, I make sure my gun is secure in the shoulder holster hidden beneath my jacket before I walk up to the back door. I make sure I have at least one weapon on me at all times. You never know when shit will hit the fan, and I'd rather be the one with a gun than without one.

Lifting my closed fist to the door, I knock three times in quick succession. A moment later, the door is pushed open, and Diego, Christian's right-hand, greets me. He looks more like a bear than human; huge, and muscular, with a face full of hair. His arms alone look like tree trunks, reminding me I should probably spend a little more time in the gym. Every inch of exposed skin is either tattooed or scared from the hundreds of fights he's been in.

"Zane," He says gruffly.

I nod my head to greet him. "Diego."

He gestures toward the hall. "Boss has been waiting for you. He's in his office." As if the boss would be anywhere else. Girls rush past me completely naked, but I don't even glance their way. I lost my appetite for other women years ago. I used to fuck girls that looked like Dove, but even that wasn't enough. There's only one fucking woman for me. And if I can't have her, I won't have anyone.

When I reach the door to Christian's office, I don't even knock. There's no point, not when he's expecting me. Opening the door, I find him sitting behind his desk, a glass of amber liquid placed in front of him. His face is blank as always, refusing to give away any emotion.

I've worked for the Sergio family since I was a teenager. He somehow got me out of prison even though I was supposed to spend a few more years behind bars. He saw something in me and let me work for him. Slowly, I worked my way up, and now I'm one of his most trusted men.

"You're late," he says. I want to tell him it's five fucking minutes, but I don't feel like arguing tonight.

"Do you have a job, or did you just call me in here so you could bust my balls?" I slam down into one of the seats in front of the mahogany desk.

"I like you, Zane, you don't walk in here with fright, or like a death sentence awaits on the other side, and you have a sense of humor."

He smiles or at least attempts to. It looks more like a grimace than anything. Christian is considerably older than me, and I think he lost the ability to smile before I was born. His black and gray hair is slicked back, and his face looks weathered, but that could be simply from doing this shit for years.

I shrug. "It's not like you're going to kill me. I'm the one dealing out death. Plus, I doubt if you wanted me dead, you would do it here."

He grabs his glass and takes a gulp of the liquid before setting the crystal glass back down. He stares at me intently—other men would be intimidated, but not me—and says, "First, I wanted to let you know that things with the Castro family are tense. They've been intercepting some of our drugs and undermining some other deals. If things continue the way they are, I might have a few jobs coming up for you. I'll need you to handle those more silently than normal. No one can know that I'm the one calling the hits."

"Okay." That's a far cry from my normal job because usually Christian likes everybody to know who is responsible for the deaths I deal out. He's known for being ruthless and killing for petty reasons. Once you're on his shitlist, your days are numbered. So, I won't deny that I'm a little curious, but not enough to ask any questions.

"That won't be a problem. Give me a list, and I'll get the job done."

"Besides the Castros, it seems like the Rossi Family is looking for a fight as well."

"Rossi, as in Xander Rossi?" I say, raising a skeptical eyebrow at him. Xander doesn't look for fights, and most know better than to fuck with him.

Christian frowns and takes a large gulp of his whiskey. He finishes the glass and slams it down onto the desk before grabbing the bottle and pouring himself another. "Yeah, the one and only."

I shouldn't ask, not that it matters, but I'm curious… far more curious than I should be. "How did you end up on his radar?"

He shakes his head like he's trying to banish away a bad dream. "It doesn't matter. What matters is staying off his radar for now. We can take care of him once I deal with the Castros, but until then, I need to stay on Xander's good side."

"Got it. Play nice with the Rossi family... *for now*."

He takes another drink. "Perfect. I do have a different job I want you to do right now, and it's a bit time-sensitive."

Where the hell are all these stipulations coming from?

"You know any job you need, I can get done. Why're you dragging your feet, Christian?"

"Your next job is a woman. I'll have Diego give you the folder with all of the details, but I need her dead within three days, and I want her body brought here. The boys will take care of it."

That little tidbit of information surprises me because typically, I have my cleanup crew take care of the bodies, but I don't say shit. Women, men, doesn't matter to me. All I see is a paycheck when I look at them, not a name, a family or a future. It's easier that way.

"Zane, have you listened to a fucking word I've said?" Christian snaps.

"Of course." I swirl the amber liquid in my glass. "Are we done here?"

"Yes, but I want you to stick around for a little fun. I got a couple new girls, and every time I offer you one, you decline. You like cock, Z? 'Cause I don't care what floats your boat. I can get you a pretty boy in here too."

"Fuck no," I sneer. "Just because I don't take up your offer doesn't mean I don't like pussy." I'm pissed that he would even say such a stupid fucking thing.

"What's the problem then? You don't like my girls? Or do you have a woman waiting for you at home?" There's a dark glint in his eyes that makes me want to smash his face into a pile of mush, but I tamp down my rage. I wouldn't ever consider telling him about Dove, not in a million years, and acting on my anger, however tempting, wouldn't be worth it.

There's always someone else to think about before I make my next move.

"Why would I have a woman in my life? They're only trouble." I say, staring at him blankly, not giving away a single thing. He thinks simply because I work for him that I'll kiss his ass and take any job he tosses my way, but what he doesn't know is I'm the real boss.

He grins. "Good, then you'll take my offer tonight. I've got a girl in one of the VIP rooms willing and waiting for you. Go blow off some steam and consider it a thank you gift for all the work you're going to be doing soon."

I consider declining, so I can go check on Dove before returning to my empty apartment, but I don't want to deal with Christian questioning me anymore. Keeping Dove a secret is essential to keeping her safe. Every single thing I do is for her, well, minus the killing; that's just to keep my impulses in check.

"Fine, you know where to find me if you need me." Pushing out of the chair, I leave his office and head in the direction of the VIP rooms.

When I enter the room, it's bathed in darkness except for a red light that's placed above a leather couch. On that couch is a naked brunette waiting for me. She smiles and climbs off the couch to walk over to me as soon as I enter the room, but I lift a hand and shake my head.

I don't plan to let the girl anywhere near me, but no one needs to know that. I'll give the woman a fat tip, and she'll keep her mouth shut, and if she doesn't... well, I'll get rid of her.

"Here's how this is going to go. I'm going to give you a couple hundred dollars, and you're going to tell your boss that we fucked, and it was great. If I find out that you tell him anything else, I'll slit your throat and watch you bleed out. Do you understand?" Her big eyes grow even bigger, and she takes a step back as if she knows being too close to me is bad.

"I swear, I won't say anything else." Her voice is as shaky as her legs.

"Sit on the couch."

"I... I won't tell anyone anything... please, please don't hurt me." She starts to cry, and I damn near lose it.

Breathing through my nose, I exhale, trying to calm myself. "I'm not going to hurt you. Not unless you don't follow my directions."

The girl doesn't say anything else and wraps her arms around her middle while watching me closely. Soft cries fill the air, but they annoy me more than anything. I've seen so many men and women cry, begging, and pleading for their lives that I'm all but immune to it.

After subjecting myself to her cries for twenty minutes, I pull out my wallet and toss two crisp hundred-dollar bills at her.

"Remember what I said..." I give her one last look before leaving the room. On my way out of the strip club, Diego hands me the folder with my next hits information. I wait until I'm in the confines of my car before I open the envelope.

The picture of the target slips from my fingers and falls to my feet. I'm about to reach for it, but then I catch the name printed in black ink before me. My heart stops, and air stills in my petrified lungs. My chest is so tight, I fear it will explode as I read the name over and over again.

No! It can't be.

5

Shawn doesn't come to work the next day, nor does he answer any of my text messages. I tell myself that it probably has nothing to do with me, but that's hard to believe when everything was fine before we agreed to go on a date.

Leaving work in a flurry, I drive across down to my therapist's office. I've been thinking more and more about stopping my appointments but haven't gotten the nerve to do it yet. They've helped a lot over the years and been a great outlet for me, but if I'm ever going to move on, I need to stop living in the past.

As I walk into Sharon's office, the hairs on the back of my neck stand on end, and a sickening feeling coats the inside of my belly. It's like tar clinging to my organs. I should be used to having this kind of feeling by now. The truth is, it never gets easier, only worse.

I wait in the waiting room, which is mostly empty, minus a man reading the paper in the corner of the room. I'm not sure why, but my attention is drawn to him, and I stare for a long time. There is something about him, but I can't pinpoint it.

He doesn't pay me any attention since he's far too focused on his paper. Unable to shake the sense of familiarity, I almost wish he would look over at me, so I can see his eyes full on. There's a pounding in my head, and my body warms all over. It's the strangest thing I've ever experienced in my life.

"Dove," Sharon calls my name, breaking the connection, and gives me a warm smile.

I stand up quickly, feeling flustered for some reason. Like I just got caught doing something I shouldn't be doing.

"Hi," I say and walk into her office. Taking my usual seat across from her, I shake whatever *that* just was off and focus on my session.

Sharon is middle-aged, divorced, and has three kids. She's been my therapist since Donna adopted me when I was a teenager, and she knows everything there is to know about me.

She stares at me, her soft eyes bleeding into mine. "How have things been?"

"Fine." I lick my lips. "I, uhh... got asked on a date."

Sharon's face lights up. "That's great. Tell me about it. How did it go?"

Defeat sits heavily on my chest. Maybe I shouldn't have started our session with this. Nonetheless, I tell her, anyway. "We never went because he never showed up. I texted him to see if he was still coming, but he never messaged back, and I haven't heard from him at all." My gaze falls to the floor. "This happens to me all the time.

Someone shows interest, and then I somehow mess it up. I don't even know what I do wrong. Whatever it is must be bad because I never hear from them again."

"How does that make you feel?"

I look up at Sharon and give her an *are you serious* look. "Like I'm not good enough, obviously. Or like something is wrong with me. Why would he not show up? Why would they never call?" I deflate against the couch with disappointment. "I would get it if they'd seen my scar or found out how messed up in my head I am, but they don't even get that far."

"There's nothing wrong with you, Dove. You know that. You have a history of always being let down, it's very normal for that to carry over into your adult life."

"No one has as much bad luck at dating as I do."

Sharon shakes her head. "How about a subject change. How is Donna doing?"

I smile at the mention of Donna. She adopted me when I had lost all hope; when I was sure I would never find someone to love me. I knew she would never be my *real* mom, but she was the closest thing I had to one. I love her, truly love her.

"Good, she's good. I try and talk to her once a week. The nursing home she's in keeps her busy." Words can't describe how glad I am that I got her into that nursing home. It's the nicest one in town, and I figured it would be too expensive, but as it turned out, Donna had some kind of insurance no one knew about that ended up paying for everything.

"Are you still having nightmares?"

A cold chill runs down my spine. I haven't had a nightmare in months, but that doesn't mean they're gone. Sometimes I go through spurts of being normal, and other times I'm so close to shattering that I'm in a constant state of fear, day and night. There is no glue to fix the broken pieces of a person's past. You can go to all the therapy sessions in the world, take all the anxiety pills there are, but sometimes nothing helps indefinitely. There are parts of me that will always be broken.

"No, the nightmares have been dormant." I fiddle with a loose string on my pants. "I went to a club the other night with Sasha. I've been trying to go out more, be a normal person, you know?" I say, sighing.

"That's good. I'm proud of you."

"The night was going well, and I was having a good time until I went to the bathroom and got separated from Sasha. I couldn't find her and…" My lip trembles at the memory of that night. How afraid I was, how fragile. It reminded me of my time in foster care. A time I'm so desperately trying to forget.

"It's okay, Dove, if you don't want to talk about it, we don't have to." Even though I'm not looking in her direction, I know she is smiling at me kindly. She always is.

"No, I want to talk about it." I swallow around the lump in my throat. "The feeling of someone watching me is at an all-time high, and I think it's because of what happened that night because I'm not talking about it."

"Okay, then continue."

Exhaling, I tell her everything from that night, how I felt when the guy touched me. How helpless I was as I rushed down the sidewalk and then how he randomly just disappeared.

I don't even realize that I've lifted my hand and been touching my scar through my shirt the whole time I've been talking. Quickly, I drop my arm and look at Sharon, who smiles at me knowingly.

"Your worry over someone watching you is very normal, especially with your history and everything that happened with that guy. If you see him again, I want you to call the police. I also want you to work on your breathing techniques. I know it's going to be hard, but try not to give in to those impulses of checking over your shoulder a million times."

I almost roll my eyes. *As if it's that easy.*

"I'll try to control my impulses, but as you can see, I'm not good at it."

"You still like to run your fingers over your scar?"

"Yes. It's just a nervous habit. I've been doing it more frequently the last few days," I admit. "I don't know why, but it calms me when I do it."

"Do you still not remember anything from that time? How you got that scar?"

"No. I don't remember anything that happened in that place." I've lied about it for so many years that the words pour out on their own. It's the only thing I've ever lied about in therapy. The only thing I never want to talk about. So, I've been sticking to my lie. I don't remember anything. The truth is, I could never forget.

The smell of alcohol and mold fills every room in this house. I've only been here for a few days, but it feels like much longer, every second in this place feels like an eternity. This is supposed to be a home for children, a safe place for me, and the other foster children to stay. There is nothing safe about this place.

My stomach growls so loud it hurts. I haven't eaten anything today, which is nothing out of the ordinary. I scour the kitchen for food, hoping that no one finds me. When I see the old granola bar wedged between empty cartons in the bottom of the pantry, I almost cry out in joy.

Grabbing the bar as fast as I can, I tuck it into the waistband of my jeans. However hungry I am, I know there is someone else here who needs food more than I do.

On tiptoes, I sneak up the stairs, avoiding the steps that I know creak. I go to the room at the end of the hallway, our room. Opening the door quietly, I hope not to wake him, but he still opens his eyes as much as he can to look at me as I enter the room. They're only open a sliver, both eyes too swollen from the beating he took before I got here.

"Hey, William," I whisper. Careful not to move the mattress too much, I crawl back into the spot beside him. "Found you some food. It's not much, but it's something."

I hand him the granola bar, and he just stares at it for a long time. He's barely talked to me since I arrived, and I'm not sure if it's because he doesn't want to or simply because he is in so much pain. He looks like he would be in a terrible amount of pain. His whole face is black and blue, swollen and scratched all over.

"You need to eat too," he finally says, handing me back the bar.

"How about we share?" I ask while opening the plastic wrapper. He sighs as if he doesn't want me to fight him on this, but then he still nods.

Taking out the bar, I break a piece off and hand it to him. Then I break an even tinier piece off for me and start nibbling on it. Most people would probably take less than thirty seconds to eat this, but we take our time. Enjoying every morsel, chewing until there is nothing left. Swallowing until each bit heavily lands in our empty stomachs.

When we're done, I hide the wrapper underneath the mattress and lie down next to him. The house is eerily quiet, which is not a good thing, maybe the calm before the storm. I close my eyes and feel around between our bodies until I find his hand. I grab it and revel in the feeling of his fingers intertwined with mine. Then I say a silent prayer, hoping that no one will come into our room tonight.

6

Zane

No matter what I do, I can't stop staring at the picture from the envelope. I don't understand why Christian would want Dove dead... how did she possibly end up on his list? Is he on to me? Watching me? Watching Dove?

I've grown more and more agitated over the last twenty-four hours. It has to be because of me. I just don't see why else she could be a target, but if it is because of me, why give me the job? Is it a test? Is he making me choose between him and her? Because no matter what, I'm always going to choose Dove.

Grinding my teeth together so hard it hurts, I look at the screen of my phone that shows me her apartment. She's sitting on the couch, curled up with a book. Not the slightest idea of the danger she is in and how drastically her life is about to change.

My head hurts from thinking about all of this. No matter how much I dig through my mind, I can't seem to find a single clear-cut answer. I better get my shit together fast because I only have three days to figure everything out.

It'd taken everything in me not to kidnap her last night and take her to the safe house I've prepared for a situation like this. I always feared that it would come to this, I just never thought it would happen this way.

I'm still ready to go, but disappearing now would put my name on top of the hitlist. No one walks away from Christian Sergio. I'm not sure what the fuck I should do next.

I need a plan. I can't go to Christian and question why Dove is on the list, not without giving myself away.

I've never questioned the people on the lists he gives me because, honestly, I've never given a fuck about any of those people. But I don't just give a fuck about Dove, she is my entire fucking world. I exist because of her. If anything were to happen to her… every muscle in my body tightens, and for one brief moment, darkness overtakes me. No. I won't let anything happen to her. I'll kill them all, every single one of them.

Exiting the app, I move to my contacts and scroll through them. The way I see it, I'm going to have to grab one of Christian's men and torture them until they tell me everything they know.

I'm already going to be number one on his shitlist when he finds out in three days that Dove isn't dead. Killing one of his men isn't going to hurt me anymore than not doing the job, so I might as well fucking do it.

Hitting the green call key, I bring the phone to my ear. The phone rings three times before Billy's deep voice fills the line.

"Hey, fucker!" *Fucker? Who does he think he is talking to?*

Swallowing my dislike for the guy, I ask, "Hey, Bill, want to grab a drink?"

"You know I can never pass on a chance to have some whiskey or beer."

I've never heard a truer statement in my life. Billy is half-drunk all the time, and when he isn't drinking, he's beating his wife.

"Let's meet at Oscars in about thirty?"

"I'll be there, Zane."

I hang up the phone without a goodbye. Billy is an easy target since he is nothing but a tech guy. That's what he does for the mob. Finds out information through hacking computers and cellphones. If anyone is going to know something, it's going to be him.

Clicking back into the app on my phone, I allow myself to check on Dove one last time. She's still sitting on the couch, immersed in her book. Without thought, I find myself stroking the screen, wishing I could touch her, taste her, feel her body against mine. I want her so badly it almost kills me. *Not yet.* I tell myself.

Closing the app once more, I shove my phone into my pocket and drive in the direction of Oscars. Since the hit was placed, I've been more cautious, looking over my shoulder, carrying an extra gun. I can't risk something happening to me and then Dove being put at risk because of it. I've worked so hard to get where I am. Worked my ass off to make sure Dove had the life she deserved, and now it's all crumbling around me.

Part of me hates myself for what I'm going to have to do while the other part of me wouldn't have it any other way. Dove is the one and only person I'm ever conflicted over. I refuse to hurt her, but my obsession with her can't be sated. I want her beside me. I want to be inside her whenever and wherever I want. For the first time ever, I want to be able to let go completely, but with only her.

Pulling into the shitty bar's parking lot, I suppress the thoughts of Dove and me sharing a future together. That can't happen if I don't get the answers I need. Which means... I need to let go. As easy as flipping a light switch off and on, I let my emotions go. Getting out of the SUV, I walk across the parking lot, the rocks crunching beneath my boots.

Walking inside the bar, the sound of loud music, laughter, and glass breaking greet me. I spot Billy in the corner of the room, looking like he's already had a few too many. *Perfect*, it should make it easier to get him to talk. I don't want to waste all my time on him.

"Hey, buddy," he slurs as I walk up to the table. As soon as I take a seat, a waitress wearing a low-cut tank top appears by my side.

"Hey, handsome, what can I get you?" she asks in a sultry tone, utterly unaware of how futile her efforts of flirting are with me.

"Beer, whatever you have on tap," I say gruffly without looking at her. She must have gotten the hint because she scurries away without another word.

For the next half an hour, I engage in friendly small talk with Billy, only sneaking in innocent questions here and there. I haven't decided if I'm going to kill him yet. It all depends on how much he knows.

"I have to say, I'm surprised you called. You never just hang out, relax, or let loose, ya know?" he says with a laugh, waving his glass around, spilling half of his beer on the table.

"What can I say? I'm turning over a new leaf. Trying to be more outgoing." The lie rolls easily off my tongue. "Especially with all these jobs, Christian has lined up for me. First, he gets into it with the Castros and now with Xander Rossi. He needs to pick his battles better; he can't fight everybody at once."

"Yeah, not sure what he was thinking, stealing those guns from Rossi. He should know better than to steal from him. This isn't the first time either... he's going to get himself killed."

I nod my head as if I already knew about the guns. Knowing this might come in handy later, but for right now, all I care to find out is what he knows about Dove.

"Yeah, not sure what he was thinking. I think he is in over his head. He has me killing all these people, and I'm still trying to figure out how I'm going to get to this chick he wants. You know, the one working at the animal shelter."

"Oh, yeah, Dove," he says, and I want to smash his face against the table just for saying her name. No one should say her name, least of all him. Licking his chapped lips, I can only imagine what he's thinking about her, "Shouldn't be too hard. She's completely unprotected." He shrugs, taking another sip of his beer before burping obnoxiously loud.

What a fucking pig.

Ignoring the impulse to slug him in the face, I say, "I wonder why the hell he would want her anyway? She seems to be a nobody."

Billy snorts. "If you only knew the half of it."

His comment has me gripping onto my glass a little tighter. Doing my best to keep my face void of all emotion, I act like I'm not interested in the subject anymore and change it.

"Anyway, I could really go for some pussy right now. Wanna head over to *Venus?* Hookers are on me tonight." I grin at him. While internally thinking about all the ways I'm about to torture him.

"Fuck yeah!" He slams the glass on the table with much more enthusiasm than necessary before getting up. Staggering over to the bar, he closes out his tab. I pay for my beer, and we both head outside.

Sucking in a lungful of fresh, crisp air, I lead Billy to my car. The idiot whistles as he gets into my SUV, completely oblivious to the fact that I'm about to torture and kill his ass.

Pulling out of the parking lot, I head toward the strip club. Billy's eyes are cast down as he plays on his phone, not noticing when I make a turn, going off route. Only when I've come to a complete stop and parked at an abandoned train station does he realize something is off.

"Where the hell are we?" He looks up and around confused. When I don't say anything, he reaches for his gun. Even without him being drunk and slow, I would have seen that move coming. It's just funny that he thinks he'll actually be able to shoot me in the condition he's in. I grab the gun from his hand with ease before he even gets the chance to point it in my direction.

"Get out," I order, pointing his own gun at him. He swallows hard and gets out slowly. As soon as I open my door, he takes off running across the parking lot. *Idiot.*

Sighing, I get out and raise the gun and pull the trigger. The bullet hits him in the leg, and he goes down with a pained groan.

"You're a fucking idiot, you know that, right?" I yell as I walk over to where he's lying. He tries to crawl away from me, but there's no hope for him now. I've drawn blood now, and I'll be the one to snuff him out.

Rearing my foot back, I kick him in the ribs, he rolls over onto his back, and I point the gun at his other leg.

"Tell me everything you know about the girl! Why does Christian want her dead?"

"You know I can't—" I cut him off by pulling the trigger. The shot rings out through the air, and another bullet rips through the flesh of his leg.

"Fucking fuck!" He's squirming around on the ground in agony, trying to get away. "I don't know why he wants her!"

I'm past playing games, now I just want the truth, want the information, so I can keep Dove safe. "Don't fucking lie to me. You already told me in the bar that you know something. Tell me and die quickly. Or I can torture you for hours. That's up to you. I've got all fucking night."

"Jesus, fuck. You can't kill me. Christian needs me, and he'll have your balls for this. I'm more useful to you alive."

"Do I look like someone who gives a fuck? At this point, you're more useful to me dead." I pull the trigger a third time. The bullet hitting him directly in his kneecap. A high-pitched scream rips from his throat, and for the next few seconds, all he does is scream. It's annoying, and I'm half tempted to shoot him in the head to make him shut up, but that wouldn't get me the information that I need.

When he is somewhat calmed down, probably because he is starting to lose a lot of blood, I ask him again, "Why does he want her dead?"

"All I know... is that..." He's fighting now to get each word out. The pain makes it hard to talk, but I don't give a shit.

"Talk!" I snarl like a dog ready to bite.

"He's been... looking for her... for a while," he groans. "For a long time."

"How long?"

"Years. Ten, maybe more."

"He has been looking for Dove for over ten years?" I have to confirm that I heard him correctly.

"Yes..."

"Why?"

"I-I don't know." He shakes his head, and I believe him. Christian's not a damn chatty man by any means, and whatever secrets he has, he keeps them close to his chest. Aiming the gun at Billy's head, I fire one last bullet, hitting him right between the eyes.

Staring down at his lifeless body for a few seconds, I try to decide if it's worth moving him. Deciding it's not, all I do is grab his wallet from his jacket and walk back to my car. I'll let the cops find him and figure something out on their own.

On the drive home, I roll down my window and throw his wallet into the river as I cross the bridge. My mind is a fucking mess as I try and connect all the dots.

Why the hell has Christian been looking for her, and why for so long? I thought Billy would be able to give me answers, but instead, he gave me more questions.

I might not have a lot of answers, but I do know one thing. I need to get Dove away from here. She's not safe anymore. Not in her own home, not at work, and definitely not anywhere in this town.

7

Dove

You know that feeling that tells you not to do something? When your gut tightens, and your palms grow sweaty. When it feels like something bad is seconds away from taking place? That's how I feel right now. Like I shouldn't be coming home, like something terrible is going to happen. I force myself to take a calming breath and unlock the door.

It's all in your head, Dove. I mean, seriously, this is my house. My home. I have no reason to be scared. Shoving the door open, I take a hesitant step inside. The hairs on the back of my neck stand on end, and goosebumps break out across my flesh.

Slowly, I close the door behind me and reach for the light switch right beside the door. It doesn't turn on, and I reach for it again, flipping the switch off and on. The light bulb must've gone out.

Feeling through the darkness, I find my way to the lamp on the side table. I flip it on, and a second later, the room is bathed in a soft glow.

Flicking my gaze around the room, I realize something is terribly off. *Max.* He's not here, and he always greets me at the door. Always...

"What the..." The words are cut off when a mammoth hand comes out of nowhere, cutting me off. A scream rips from my throat, but the sound is muffled beneath the hand that's pressed firmly against my lips. Pulled back against a firm chest, a thick arm of muscle wraps around my middle, restraining me completely. All I feel is a hard body against my back as I'm practically carried away from the door.

Panic like I've never felt before rises up inside of me, and instantly I start to struggle, my fight or flight instincts kicking in. Those instincts do me no good when the man holding onto me is so much bigger and stronger than I am. Fighting is a waste of strength and effort, two things I'm already lacking. Tears prick my eyes and hot breath fans against my ear.

I wasn't wrong. Someone was watching me, and now he's got me. Now he's going to hurt me. Rape me and kill me. He's going to get what he wanted all along.

Kicking out my legs, the heel of my foot lands against my assailant's shin, and a grunt fills my ears. The kick isn't enough for him to release me though, so I continue fighting. I won't be a helpless victim again. I won't let him hurt me without a fight.

A million scenarios run through my head. Opening my mouth, I feel his flesh against my lips, and it hits me then what I need to do. What I should've done all along.

Biting into the meaty flesh of his palm, I sink my teeth deep like a dog and don't let go, not until he forcefully pulls his hand away.

"Fuck," he growls. The timbre of his voice is deep and frightening, and fear blankets my insides. I do my best to tamp that fear down, but it reminds me of a time when I was helpless and had no one. Putting everything I can into getting away, I let out a horrid scream, knowing this is probably my one and only chance of having someone hear me.

Instantly, his hold disappears and shock courses through me as I twist around coming face to face with my attacker. *Is this a game to him?* I don't understand why he let me go, maybe to leave me feeling hopeful?

Flattening myself against the wall, I look at him. He's tall and handsome, and for one single second, I'm stunned like a deer seconds away from death. Standing there, I stare at the man who has been following me.

The same man who was sitting in Sharon's waiting room with me hours ago.

He lifts his hands, and I flinch. "I'm not going to hurt you. I would never hurt you," he says. His words don't match his actions though, and when I look into his eyes, I see emptiness. I see someone without a conscious, without the ability to feel. It chills me to the bone. I feel like prey caught in a trap, and here right in front of me is a predator.

Taking a step to the side, I slide along the wall. My gaze flicks to the door and then back to him. If I want to get out of here alive, I'm going to have to be fast. He's definitely stronger than me, but I might be faster, especially if I can catch him off guard. I don't care if he says he's not going to hurt me. I need to get out. Get away from him.

All I can hear is my heartbeat hammering in my ears. A rush of fear ripples through me as he takes a step forward, partially blocking the front door. My throat closes, and it feels like an elephant is sitting on my chest.

Run. Escape. I internally scream at myself, but it feels like my feet have blocks of concrete attached to them. Snapping out of it, I turn on my heels and rush toward the kitchen. If I can just get a knife or something to fight him off. I toss anything and everything in my path at him, but nothing deters him, and I don't make it far before he catches me. His hand wraps around my wrist, and he tugs me backward, causing my body to collide with his chest. The air is forced from my lungs with the impact.

His strength is a reminder that I am nothing more than a fly in the fight against him. Wrapping both arms around me, almost as if he's giving me a bear hug, he picks me up and presses me to the nearest wall.

"Please, don't, please..." I start to beg.

"Shhh," he murmurs softly. The man's face is millimeters away from mine, and I can feel his harsh heartbeat through the thin material of his shirt, the clean scent of soap invading my senses.

He releases his hold on me, but I'm still trapped between him and the wall with nowhere to go. No escape. Fear wraps around my throat like a shackle. Lifting a hand to my trembling face, he cups my cheek and gently swipes away the tears. I wasn't even aware they'd started falling from my eyes.

"I would never ever hurt you. You are way too important to me, Dove. You have to trust me, I promise everything is going to be okay." He tries to soothe me, but not a single part of me believes him. My mind is racing, and I have a thousand questions. Why else would he break into my house and attack me if he wasn't going to hurt me? How does he know my name? And most importantly, why am I important to him? He must have the wrong person. This is all a big misunderstanding.

I'm shaking now, consumed with fear, and my vision is blurry with tears.

"Stop," he orders, slamming a fist into the wall beside my head. His voice is harsh and only makes me cry harder. He seems to grow frustrated by my failure to listen and releases a hard sigh a moment later. "I didn't want to have to do this to you... but you've left me no choice."

He takes a step closer, and we're so close now that we are chest to chest. Our faces are only inches apart. My eyes are in line with his full lips, and that's when I realize just how much taller he is. Out of the corner of my eye, I see him reaching for something, and I know this has to be it. The end is near, after all I've been through in my life, this is how it's going to end.

"I'm sorry," I whimper, and even in the face of death, I'm unable to stop the tears from coming. I want to fight, but it's as if there isn't anything left in me.

I'm barely hanging on, barely breathing, barely here. I flinch when he leans into me and buries his face into my hair. The action is so intimate, and when I hear him inhale sharply like he's smelling me, a shiver skids down my spine.

"No, it's me who is sorry, Dove," he whispers against my ear a moment before I feel a pricking sensation against my neck and something cold entering my skin.

"Don't...please..." I try and get the words I want to say out, but my thoughts become hazy. Muddled. Up and down become the same.

Leaning away from me, his face once again comes into view, his full lips a breath away from my own. Strangely, I find he's beautiful as he peers down at me. Beautiful and frightening, all at the same time.

"Shhh, everything is going to be okay now. You'll always be safe in my arms." He threads his fingers through my hair and brings our foreheads together. He holds my head in place, forcing me to stare into his dark, cold eyes.

I'm fading fast and find that most of my body sags against his now. My heartbeat slows, and my lips part, and I want to ask him how I'm going to be safe with him? The words never come though; my tongue is too heavy to talk.

"It's okay, don't be afraid..." His voice is the last thing I hear, and his haunting eyes the last thing I see as the world fades to complete darkness.

8

Zane

P art of me knows what I did to her is wrong and fucked up. But I couldn't help myself. What other choice did I have anyway? If I don't disappear with her, Christian will find her and have someone else kill her.

Having her in my arms, even with fear in her eyes was everything I thought it would be and more. Her soft body molded against mine perfectly, her sweet scent surrounded me, and feeling the rapid beat of her heart against mine was the best kind of high.

When she started crying, I snapped, her tears are a trigger to me. I hate seeing her cry, but even with her tears, I can't seem to shut off my body's reaction to her. My cock grew harder than steel, and I had to stop myself from taking from her, reminding myself that she is fragile and that if I did something, I might regret it. *No*, I would definitely regret it.

The drive to the safe house seems to take forever, and I find myself glancing between Dove's sleeping body and the road over and over again.

With every mile, we leave the city further and further behind. I stop once to switch cars. Luckily, I had parked the getaway car in a parking garage, so no one saw me as I dragged Dove's unconscious body from one vehicle to the other.

Soon enough, I'm pulling into the driveway of what looks like an ordinary farmhouse. The white picket fence has seen better days, and the siding on the house needs to be power washed. The paint on the porch is chipped, and the windows look like they haven't been cleaned in years. It looks like no one has lived here in some time, but it's not about what you see on the outside but what lurks inside.

When I bought this place, it wasn't because of the farmhouse, but because of what was underneath it. The house was built on top of an old 1960's bunker. The house itself was nothing more than a cover-up. I gutted the entire place, made it bigger, and homey, knowing that someday I may have to bring Dove here. I wanted her to be happy here, on the off chance that we ever got to a place where we could be together.

Parking, I turn the car off and sit there for a long second. Normally, I can shut off my emotions and let go completely. This is different. In order to protect Dove and ensure I don't hurt her, I can't shut down. I have to keep myself in check.

That means I have to learn to deal with the feelings I'm having right now. Which is hard as fuck because all I want to do is strip her bare and take until there's nothing left. All my sick and twisted dreams have come true, but only at the expense of Dove's life.

Remember that, asshole.

I may have finally gotten her, but I'll die before I let anyone hurt her. Things have just gotten ten times more complicated. Not only will I have to protect her from Christian, but I'll have to protect her from myself.

I walk around the SUV to the passenger side and open the door. Taking her body into my arms, I cradle her protectively against my chest. She weighs hardly anything, and I don't like it, not one fucking bit. I'll need to plump her up a bit before I consider fucking her. The last thing I want is to break her. Right then, an image of my sweet little Dove broken—her beautiful face stricken with pain—fills my mind.

I can't let that happen, ever.

The sun has just started rising, illuminating the house with an orange glow as I carry her inside. The floor creaks as I walk up the porch, unlocking the front door of the house. Gripping onto her a little tighter, I manage to punch in the code to the keypad leading downstairs. There's a loud beep, and then the door opens.

I walk inside and close it behind me before descending the stairs. The basement is expansive, with a full-sized kitchen, master bedroom, living room, a library, a gym, and a master suite with a jetted tub and a full floor to ceiling shower. When I had this place redone, I wanted to be sure that Dove would be comfortable here, especially if we have to stay for a while, which at this time looks that way.

Heading straight to the bedroom, I deposit her gently on the silk sheets and brush a few strands of dark brown hair off her face. *Angelic.* Part of me feels like this is nothing but a dream, that there's no way she's here, and mine to do with as I please.

I let my gaze move lower and stop on the exposed skin of her abdomen where her shirt has ridden up. Smooth, creamy white flesh taunts me, and I drag two knuckles over it, reveling in the warmth and pleasure it ignites deep inside me.

I've wanted this forever... for as long as I can remember. I just want her. The thick rod between my legs twitches, and I nearly chuckle. He, too, has wanted this forever, and soon enough, he'll get a taste, but for now, we'll both have to do with my hand.

Forcing myself to move away from the bed, I walk out into the living room and make my way back upstairs. Going back out to the car, I gather all the bags I packed, then I get the travel crate out of the back that has Max in it. He starts meowing as soon as he sees me.

"I'll get you out in a minute," I say, realizing then that I just talked to a cat.

I carry everything downstairs in two trips, before double and triple-checking all the locks. When I get back into the bedroom, Dove still hasn't moved. Not that I expected her too. I gave her quite a strong sedative. I wouldn't be surprised if she sleeps for the rest of the day.

Allowing myself to touch her face one last time, I cradle her cheek and press a kiss to the crown of her forehead before breaking away to take a shower.

Pulling out some clean towels, I walk into the bathroom and strip out of my clothing before turning the shower on. As soon as the room starts to fill with steam, I step beneath the spray. Leaning against the tile, I let the water beat down on my tired muscles.

My cock is still harder than steel, and my balls are aching, begging me for release. The image of her in my bed doesn't help matters and only makes me crave the warmth of her body more. Taking myself into my hand, I give the rod a hard stroke, causing a hiss of pleasure to slip past my lips. Repeating the stroke, a little harder this time, I rub my thumb over the slit at the head of my cock.

Fuck. Letting my eyes drift closed, I envision my hand as Dove's pussy, my hips thrusting forward, my cock moving in and out of her furiously, claiming her like I've always wanted to. Squeezing myself a little harder, I picture her clenching around me, her lips parted, her cheeks red, and her beautiful eyes frenzied with heat. Thrusting into my hand a little harder and faster at the image, it doesn't take long before I explode.

Ropes of sticky come leave my cock and land against the tile before the water washes it away. I barely keep myself standing upright, the orgasm rocking me straight to the core. I've lost count of how many times I've allowed my mind to wander like this, to use Dove as an image to jack off to. I've seen her naked on camera so often, I know every curve of her nude body, but I've never got the chance to feel them, never got to touch her soft skin.

It's almost too tempting now, I have her here with me, and I'm no longer forced to hold back. Soon enough, I'll be giving us both the pleasure we desperately deserve.

Finishing up my shower, I wash my body and hair and then rinse.

When I'm done, I get out and dry off before wrapping the towel around my waist. Walking back into the bedroom, my eyes immediately fall on the sleeping form on the bed. My gaze never wavers as I drop the towel and start getting dressed. Even though I just came, my dick is already stirring back to life again. *Shit*, I need to get a grip.

Trying to keep myself occupied and my mind anywhere but on Dove, I unpack the bags I brought and get everything else situated. Once done, I take a seat on the edge of the bed and stare at her. Now I just have to wait for my sleeping beauty to wake up.

9

Dove

The first thing I notice when I wake is the pain radiating through my head. It feels like someone is trying to pry my skull open. The second thing is the silky sheets my cheek is pressed against, and that alone gives me enough steam to force my heavy lids open.

For one single moment, all I am is confused, then like a freight train, the events come rushing back to me. All the confusion is shoved aside as fear and panic overtake me.

Eyes as black as night. The prick of a needle in my neck. Promises of love.

My stomach churns, and a wave of dizziness slams into me as I scan the room, my gaze darting around, looking for an exit, for *him*. When I don't see anyone, I look down at my body and find that I'm still completely clothed.

Thank god for that.

There's no soreness between my legs as I move to the edge of the bed, so I feel confident enough that he didn't rape me. Lifting my hands to my face, I feel around for any bumps or bleeding. I don't find any wounds, and I don't feel any pain besides the soreness in my neck and the splitting headache I have, so I'm thankful for that.

Overall, I seem to be fine at the moment, but that's not a complete relief because I have no clue where the hell I am or how I'll get out of here. On top of that, I don't even know where my captor is. Or if there is more than one of them.

Another wave of fear slams into me, threatening to immobilize me. There has to be more than one of them. It's just not possible that this was done alone. Who can just kidnap someone from their home and take them god knows where without anyone noticing them?

God, this is so bad, and something tells me it's not going to get any better.

Frantically, I get up and start pacing around the room. It's pretty luxurious, with a large king-sized bed and expensive-looking furniture. Two bedside lamps give the room all its light. *It still must be night.* Heavy curtains are draped over the windows. *Windows...*

Rushing across the room, I grab two fistfuls of the curtains and pull them open. I suck in a sharp breath when I see what's behind them. *Bricks.* They're just bricks. It's a sham, a damn facade. I check the other window and find the same kind of brick wall behind it. Then the third, as if that one would be any different. Still, there is a small sliver of hope that lives inside me, which is crushed as soon as I pull the last set of curtains away.

Bile rises in my throat, and I press a hand to my stomach. I think I'm going to be sick. I'm trapped... in some kind of basement. Digging my nails into the palm of my hand, I swallow down the vomit and focus my attention.

I need to find a way out.

There are two doors, both are closed, so I have no idea where they lead or what lurks behind them. Taking a deep breath, I walk over to the first one. Fear trickles slowly into my veins. Hesitantly, I reach for the doorknob, my fingers curl around the cold metal, and I turn it. Thinking the door is probably locked, I don't expect it to open, so when it does, a surprised gasp falls from my lips. I stand there shocked for all of two seconds before I walk out into the huge open space.

I'm trapped in a god damn, underground apartment, a giant one at that. My apartment would probably fit three times in this room alone. I try and act like I don't care, but this place is something else.

I stare out into the living room, where a large sectional couch, an entertainment center with a TV the size of a small theater screen is.

A dining area sits in the center of the space, with a table that seats six. A large colorful flower centerpiece ties the room together, giving it a homey feel.

The entire place leaves me feeling completely confused. It's almost like someone lives here... It's far too nice of a place for a prisoner to live in, which makes me wonder if I'm really a prisoner here or something else entirely.

The kitchen is on the other side of the room, with modern-looking cabinets and stainless-steel appliances. Then it dawns on me. There's a fully functioning kitchen, and a kitchen means knives, which I can use as a weapon. Carelessly, I rush from the bedroom and into the kitchen. My hands are shaking as I search the counters for a knife block.

Opening the drawers, my hope splinters as I only find spoons and forks, but not a single knife. Desperate, I grab a fork just to feel like I have something I could do damage with. With my free hand, I continue to open the drawers hoping maybe something will appear.

When nothing does, the panic starts to set in again. Oh, god. I'm trapped in this basement, with nothing more than a fork to protect myself with. Running a hand through my hair, I will my out of control heartbeat to slow down.

Think, Dove, think.

"Are you looking for something?" That deep voice pierces the fog around my mind, and I whirl around, raising my arm in front of me and pointing the fork in the direction of the voice. My eyes find the nameless guy that took me from my apartment. Inky black hair, and eyes the color of charcoal add to the dark vibe he's got going on.

Dragging my gaze down his body, I find he's wearing nothing more than a pair of low hanging basketball shorts. His broad, muscled chest is on display, and beads of sweat drip down it, leaving a trail behind.

Why is he sweating? Why am I staring?

I force myself to look away from his chest. I don't care what he looks like, he kidnapped me. Peering up into his eyes, I find he's staring me down, the dark orbs twinkle with a sliver of amusement when he spots the fork in my hand.

The blood in my veins turns to ice at the darkness I see in his eyes. There is no light, no good, and that scares me almost more than what's happening because if he has no conscience, no reason to care, then I'm as good as dead.

"Let me go!" I order, cutting the fork through the air like a knife.

He grins, literally grins at me like I'm an adorable kitten, instead of a woman willing to do whatever she can to get free.

"Do you truly think you can hurt me with a fork?" he says, and it feels like a taunt, which only angers me more.

"There is no thinking about it. If you don't let me go, I will stab you with this fork." I make my voice sound strong and tighten my grip on the end. My palms are sweaty, and I'm scared. So damn scared. The last time I was this scared, I was sure that creeper was going to get me, and I refuse to let something bad happen again. If I have to, I'll save myself.

He takes a threatening step toward me, and my muscles quake. My brain is telling me to run, ordering me to, but looking at the man before me, there is no way I'll get around him, and even if I do, I have no idea where I'll go.

"Put the fork down before you hurt yourself. I told you I wasn't going to hurt you, and I meant it." He speaks gently to me like I'm a child, and I stare at him with confusion. His words don't match his actions. His voice is a soft whisper and doesn't match the devil persona he's giving off. I can only assume this is some sick game to him.

"Not *yet*... you're not hurting me yet, but you will. I'm not stupid. Why else would you kidnap me and lock me in a basement? Let me go, and I won't call the police. I won't tell anyone about what happened."

"I'm sorry, but I can't do that, Dove," he says, frowning and taking another step toward me. He lifts his hand, and I flinch, taking a step back to keep the distance between us.

"Can't and won't aren't the same thing." I look over his shoulder, trying to plan out my next move. It's a mistake and one that'll cost. He moves with lightning speed toward me. *He's going to kill me.* All I can do is gasp as he grabs the wrist with the fork in it and squeezes hard enough to cause me to release it.

It falls to the floor, the sound of the metal bouncing across the tile fills the space. As if his touch burns my skin, I tug my arm out of his hold. His dark eyes narrow, and he looks at me like he wants to grab my hand again, but he refrains. *Who is he? Why does he want me?*

"Please, just let me go, please!" Panic is clawing at my insides.

Something resembling remorse flashes across his face but is soon replaced with an emotionless mask.

"Come, I'll show you around, and if you behave, I'll let you go into the library."

Library? How can he act so normal, like nothing is wrong? Like he isn't breaking the law? He has got to be out of his damn mind if he thinks I'm following him anywhere.

Lost in my thoughts, I forget he's standing here, watching me, staring like he can see deep inside my soul. An involuntary shiver ripples down my back.

"You're insane, psychotic." I cross my arms over my chest, trying to make myself appear big when I feel like a tiny mouse trapped in a trap. "I'm not going anywhere with you. I'm not staying here. Just let me go. Whatever you want, I don't have it. If it's money or something, I have none. I have nothing, you chose the wrong girl."

His lips twitch as if he wants to smile. "I've been called worse in my life, and I've most definitely chosen the right girl. I don't want your money, Dove." Taking another step, he crowds me. My heart thunders in my chest, and I bite the inside of my cheek to stop myself from crying out. The coppery tang of blood fills my cheek. He's close enough for me to touch him now, and his nearness terrifies me almost as much as his distance. When he leans into my face, I catch a whiff of sweat, soap, and just man, "All I want is you, and now I have you. Right where I want you, so relax and let me show you around your new home."

"My... my new home?" My lips tremble as I speak, and he pulls back a little, his eyes studying my face. Heat blooms in my cheeks at the inspection.

"Yes, your new home. I hope you're happy with the accommodations. I wanted to be sure you are as comfortable as possible. I even brought Max since I know you love him so much."

"M-Max?" I'm shocked. Shocked and terrified and confused. The reality of everything sinks in very slowly, and I realize then what I should've realized all along. Whoever this guy is, he's never going to let me go.

10

Zane

Max must have heard us talking about him because, on cue, he appears in the kitchen. He purrs loudly as he wraps his body around the corner of the cabinet. Dove bends down to pick him up, holding him to her chest protectively. I do my best to understand her fear, but she should know better.

"If I really wanted to hurt you, I could've easily done so when you were knocked out." I point out the obvious, but it seems to fall on deaf ears.

Although the whole *I'll stab you with a fork* thing was quite adorable and turned me on a little bit. It's cute that she thinks she can fight me off, that she can escape.

"I... I can't stay here. No." She shakes her head, strands of hair fall onto her face, and she looks up at me with panic in her blue eyes. "I won't stay here. You can't make me. I... I'll scream. I'll fight you. I will not let you keep me here."

Each word is like a lash against my heart. Her words hurt me more than I expected them to. I knew she would want to escape, to fight me, but I never expected her to be so strong-willed. I realize instantly that I need to try a different approach, or I'm going to have to drug her again and tie her to the bed.

"Would it help you if I told you my name?"

Her eyes widen, and she looks shocked. "No! I don't care about your name. I don't care about any of this. I just..." She pauses and then darts forward, dropping Max in the process to run away from me. Like cats do, he lands on his feet and lets out a hiss as he scurries away.

Jesus Christ. This is turning out to be a shitshow. Now I'm going to have to do the one thing I don't want to do. Her panic is out of control, and the only thing that's going to keep her in line and make her see through the fog is fear.

I hate the idea of deceiving her like this, of threatening her, but it's my last option before drugging her again.

"I tried to be kind, tried to reason with you, but my patience is wearing thin." My voice drops and turns menacing as I chase after her. Without having a clue as to where she's going, she runs back into the bedroom, basically trapping herself. Her determination is almost comical. She tries to shut the door behind her, but I block it with my foot.

"Please…" The anguish in her voice calls to me. It begs for my protection, but there's no protecting her from me. At least not right now.

Like a trapped and wounded animal, she rushes around the bed, hiding on the other side. Ha, like a piece of furniture could protect her from me. I'll rip the fucking thing apart piece by piece. Vibrating with frustration, I try to talk myself off the ledge.

My gaze collides with hers, and the softest whimper I've ever heard escapes her lips as I prowl toward the bed. She doesn't know how dangerous this is for her. How easy it would be for me to let go and ruin everything.

There's nothing to stop me from falling off the edge, no one to hold me back.

Standing next to the bed, her eyes dart to the door and back to me again. Back and forth, they move like a bouncy ball, and without her even knowing, she's giving herself away.

I'm trained to kill, trained to see peoples' next move. She's a chessboard, and her face is giving away her next move.

Walking a little further into the room, I say, "If you don't stop running from me, you'll force my hand. You're going to make me do something I'd rather not. I'm not a monster, Dove, but I'll do what I have to, to prove my point."

"I'm not scared of you," she yells across the bed, her cheeks red. The tremble in her voice, giving away the lie.

Shaking my head, I walk around the bed. Her eyes scan the room, and with nowhere else to go, she climbs up onto it. If my next move doesn't work, I'll have to subdue her with my body.

"If you don't stop, I'll visit your friend from the shelter. Sasha...is it?" As soon as the words leave my lips, she freezes in the center of the bed. "Or maybe I'll visit Donna at the New Haven Senior Care."

My threat hangs heavy in the air as I watch Dove's face pale. She might act brave and fearless when it comes to her own safety, but she won't risk the lives of the people she loves. She doesn't know I wouldn't actually hurt them.

Not since I know how important those people are to her. Not knowing how well Donna took care of her and how good of a friend Sasha has been to her.

Fresh tears pool in her eyes, and when she blinks, they slide down her cheeks.

"Don't... don't hurt them. Please, I'll do whatever you want. Just don't hurt them."

I should feel satisfied with myself as I watch her drop down onto the mattress, her cheeks stained with sadness, but I hate that I had to go there.

"I won't hurt them unless you make me. Now, I want to show you around the house. This doesn't have to be a prison, it's all what you make of it. Will you behave now?"

She nods and hesitantly crawls off the bed, her head lowered in defeat as she comes to stand next to me.

"Now that we've gotten that out of the way. I'm Zane. I built this entire place for you. The library, gym, living room. Every inch of this place was built with you in mind."

That seems to get her attention, and she looks up from the floor and right at me.

"Why would you build this place for me? I don't even know you." I ignore her question, knowing that answering one will lead to a million more.

"Come, let me show you around." I extend my hand, and she looks at it with hesitation before placing her own in mine. Pleasure sparks deep in my gut and radiates south into my cock. Her hand is so tiny, fragile, and warm. Before I let my brain drag me in a different direction, I start the tour.

"This is the master bedroom, which we'll share together. Through that door," I point to the far-right door. "That's the bathroom. There is a huge shower, and a tub for you to soak in since I know you like your baths."

Her eyes go impossibly wide, and I can only imagine what's going on in her head right now. Tugging her out of the bedroom, I walk toward the living room. "You already know where the kitchen and dining room are. Here is the living room. I've got all your favorite movies and tv shows here." She doesn't say a thing just stares open-mouthed at the space.

"Off the living room is a short hallway, which leads to the gym and library." I point in the direction of the hall.

Turning to me, she looks up at me, her wet lashes fanning against her cheek. "W-why would you do this, and how do you know what I like and don't like?"

Part of me wants to tell her nothing, to remain silent, but eventually, she'll know the truth. Eventually, she'll find out just how important she is to me.

I tug her closer and grip her gently by the hip, loving the way she molds like clay to my will. "Because, Dove, I've been watching you. I know everything about you. What you like, what you don't like. Your favorite foods, movies, what time you wake up in the morning. I even know when you get your period and for how long it lasts."

Shock, fear, confusion, it all blends into one on her face.

"Y-you watched me?" She's trembling now, and I know it's not because she's cold.

"Yes, for a long time." I can't help but smile. Yes, she's afraid now, but soon she'll come to realize she has nothing to be afraid of, that everything I did was for her.

"W-Why?"

"I told you. Because I care for you, and I want you to be safe."

"I... I think I'm going to be sick." She lifts a hand to her mouth, and I release her, watching as she runs away from me and in the direction of the bathroom. I follow behind her and walk in to see her hunched over the toilet. Gently, I pull her hair back away from her face as she empties her stomach contents into the bowl.

"Shhh, it's okay." I soothe, using my other hand to rub up and down her back.

"It's not okay," she whispers, "none of this is okay." Her body goes rigid.

I'm tempted to tighten my hold on her hair a little bit, but I don't want to hurt her. That's the last thing I want. There will be time for the things I want later, but right now, Dove needs me. She needs my kindness.

"It might not make sense, or be okay right now, but eventually, you'll come to terms with it. Change is hard."

Pulling away, the silky strands of her hair fall through my fingers as she scurries back against the side of the tub. Wiping at her mouth with the back of her sleeve, she peers up at me with confusion.

"I don't understand. I don't know why I'm here or why I'm important to you or what any of this is. I just want to go home. Please, let me go home." Tears well in her eyes again, tugging at my heartstrings, but I banish the thoughts away.

I am her home, forever, and for always.

"This is your home now, and it will be so until I say otherwise. Now, when you're ready, you can come out and join me for dinner." I want to take her into my arms, hold her and make her forget about the fear but it's too soon. Instead, I do the only thing I can. I put some distance between us because like the old saying goes: Distance makes the heart grow fonder.

11

Dove

Zane walks out of the bathroom, leaving me alone with my thoughts, All I can do is sag against the vanity.

The things he knows about me are terrifying and completely unnatural. It's not normal to know how someone takes their coffee when you have not spent any time with that person. Nothing is normal about any of this, how can he not see how crazy this is?

I'm exhausted and afraid of what's to come. He's been watching me... and the things that he knows. I bite my lip to stifle a whimper. I have to get it together and try to escape this prison.

Forcing myself to use the breathing techniques Sharon taught me, I back away from the ledge of fear and analyze the information I have. He's not going to let me go, that much is obvious. It's clear he has an obsession of some sort with me, but he doesn't want to hurt me, or at least it seems that way right now.

Hugging my knees to my chest, I do my damnedest to try and come up with a solution, a way out, but there isn't one. There is nothing, and that leaves me feeling hopeless and ten times more afraid.

"Dove." He calls my name from a distance, and then I hear him moving around, his feet barely make any noise. A moment later, he appears in the doorway, still shirtless.

"Dinner is ready."

Shit. How long have I been sitting here?

Pushing myself up from the floor, I come to stand in front of him. A ghost of a smile appears on his lips before he turns around and walks out.

I follow him through the apartment, watching the muscles of his back move with every step he takes. I'm so mesmerized by them that I don't realize when we've made it to the dining room table until he stops abruptly, and I slam right into his back.

He spins around and grabs me by the forearms to steady me. His touch is gentle, warm, and makes me feel weird. Like he shouldn't be kind to me.

"Sorry."

"Nothing to be sorry about," he says, his voice softer now. "Sit down. You must be hungry." Now that he's mentioned it, yes, I'm starving. Though I'm not going to tell him that.

Looking at the table, I see that he's already prepared two bowls of what looks to be some kind of hearty soup. Taking a seat, I let the savory smell invade my nose, causing my stomach to growl loudly.

"All we have is canned goods right now, no meat and no fresh produce. I wanted to be here when you woke up. That's why I didn't leave to get it earlier. Since you're up now and know where everything is, I'm going to make a quick supply run after we eat."

Bringing the spoon to my mouth, I pause. "You're going to leave me here?"

"Yes, there is no need to worry. You'll be completely safe here. No one is getting in."

"Or out?"

"No, you won't be able to leave without me." He confirms what I already knew before adding. "But that's for your own protection." Like it's important, I know that or something.

"You keep saying you're trying to protect me, but you never say from who or what?"

His eye twitches, and I swear I see the cold mask of indifference fall back over his face. "Let's not talk about that now. You need to eat. I can hear your stomach from here."

Shoving the spoon into my mouth, I bite back a groan as the soup lands against my tongue. I don't care if it's canned soup it tastes like heaven right now. In a matter of minutes, I have my entire bowl eaten. Zane eats slowly, watching each and every bite I take, like it's the most entertaining thing in the world.

"You're staring at me."

Zane shrugs. "I like watching you."

I swallow down the witty come back, and instead, get up and take my stuff into the kitchen. Placing the dirty dishes in the sink, I lean against the counter, trying to figure out what I'm supposed to do now.

Shoving out of the dining room chair, he walks into the kitchen, and my eyes gravitate toward him. I try not to look at his perfectly sculpted stomach, or each ab that's on display and definitely not the deep V partially hidden by his low hanging shorts.

"I'm going to clean this up, get dressed, and then leave. Do you need anything while I'm out?" he asks, and I swear I can hear the smirk in his voice.

"No." Staring down at the floor, I shake my head.

"Are you sure? This might be the last time I'll go out for a while. We need to lay low for the next few weeks."

What does that mean?

"What am I supposed to do while you're gone?"

"Whatever you want. This is your home too. Watch some tv, read a book, or take a bath." He tosses out suggestions like he didn't just kidnap me and threaten people I care about.

"Okay." I move out of the kitchen as he cleans up. Slowly, I walk into the living room and sit down on the sectional. Sinking into the leather, I wish I could enjoy it, but I'm too tense. My stomach churns, and I press a hand to it to keep the nausea inside at bay. Zane walks into the bedroom, and a moment later, returns fully dressed.

He stops directly in front of me and squats down, bringing us eye to eye. I try to avert my gaze, but trying to look anywhere else is impossible with him right in front of me. "I'm going to leave now. I'll be back before you know it. Don't do anything stupid while I'm gone. Please. I don't want to have to threaten you again, or worse, follow through on my threat."

Chewing on my bottom lip, I nod. What the hell could I possibly do anyway?

"Good." He smiles and then leans forward, pressing a kiss to my forehead. His lips burn where they touch my skin, and something strange erupts inside me. It's foreign and confusing, and I don't understand it because, in a strange way, that simple gesture is comforting to me. At the same time, it's sickening too because I shouldn't feel anything close to comfort from this man. He's my captor, not my roommate or friend.

Leaving me sitting on the couch, he walks up the stairs and pauses at the top. Leaning forward, I curiously watch as the door opens, and he walks out. Not even a second later does the door close heavily behind him. As soon as I'm alone, my chest feels heavy. I'm trapped and alone. Complete quiet blankets the room. All I can hear is the swooshing of blood in my ears and my own soft breathing.

Do something! My brain screams. He said it will be a while before he leaves again, so this might be my only chance.

∽

I SPEND the next two hours looking for a way out of here while trying to find things I could possibly use as weapons. With each passing minute, my hope diminishes. My first thought was to get a weight from the gym, but of course, that was the only door that was locked. I beat my fists against the door for a while before giving up.

The fork was pretty much the best protection I could find. The second thing I found was a lamp with a heavy bottom. Taking off the shade, I do a few trial swings with it. *I can do this.* My anxiety is through the roof. I've never hurt a person before, never punched someone, never drew blood, and now I'm about to try and take out a guy bigger than me with a lamp.

A few minutes later, I hear the door at the top of the stairs open. Oh, god. With the lamp clamped tightly in my hand, I scurry across the room and hide next to the stairs. I flatten myself against the wall and say a silent prayer. My heart is pounding so loudly I fear he might hear it. Sweat forms against my palms as I adjust my grip while listening to him descend the steps.

You can do this. It's this or nothing.

His body comes into view, and I see that his arms are full of grocery bags. *Perfect.* Shutting all rational thinking down, I move out of my hiding spot and swing the lamp at his head just as he turns in my direction.

I catch him across the face instead of the back of the head like I had planned. The lamp smashing into the side of his face.

Shit! My hands tremble as I drop the lamp to the floor at the same time, he drops the grocery bags. I take an instinctive step back when he lifts a hand to his face in slow motion. When he pulls his hand away, I see red on his fingers.

Blood. He's bleeding. My lungs burn, and I freeze. The look in his eyes is murderous, rooting me in place and turning the blood in my veins to ice. All I can think is, this is it, this is where he kills me. Where he beats me and ties me to the bed. Where I die a slow, painful death.

"Fuck, I told you to be good." He's almost growling like an animal, his lip is curled as he takes a threatening step toward me.

"Please." I lift my hands to protect my face because I know what's coming. I know he's going to hurt me. Bracing for the pain, I grit my teeth and squeeze my eyes shut.

Except the pain never comes. Instead, he tenderly grabs my hands and lowers them while gently nudging me backward. In that moment, fear roots me to the floor, and I'm not sure I could scream or run away even if I wanted to. When my back collides with the wall, the air in my lungs expels, and I know I'm trapped.

I haven't known my captor long, but I already know that with him, I'm always trapped. I look anywhere but at his face. I don't want to see the cut or the bruise on his cheek. I'm not a violent person, and I hate that this situation has made me into someone I'm not.

His hand comes out of nowhere, and I flinch as he pinches my chin between two fingers, forcing me to look into his eyes. Dark black pools of nothingness reflect back at me.

If there is anything I've learned about Zane, it's that he is unreadable. Like a lake, you can't see the bottom, but you know there's something there beneath the surface. Lurking in the dark, deep waters. You just aren't sure what it is. That's Zane.

Releasing my chin, he drags his knuckles over my cheek before he cups it. The gesture is gentle, kind, and it confuses me. I'd expected his rage, his anger, fury, but kindness? No way.

"It doesn't matter what you do to me, Dove. I will never put my hands on you in any way to cause you harm. I will never hurt you." He leans into me, so close that I can feel his hot breath on my lips.

This strange heat blooms in my belly, and my gaze darts from his eyes and down to his full lips and back again. I'm riding a teeter-totter of emotions and toeing the line between what is right and wrong. This is wrong, bad. I want to kiss him, to let him consume me, to taste his venom on my lips, but I don't understand why. I'm terrified, but also curious. I shouldn't let my captor kiss me or touch me, but a very strange part of me craves him.

As if he can read my mind, his lips descend on mine. Lifting my hands, I rest them against his chest. Do I want to stop him? My brain says, push him away, but my heart tells me to hold him close. My entire body trembles at the gentle brush of his top lip over mine before his bottom lip caresses mine.

Though the kiss is soft, nothing more than a whisper, the intensity of it steals the air from my lungs. It evokes an emotion from deep within that I haven't felt for years.

Safe. Protected.

The smell of clean soap and the warmth of his body clings to me. My ribs are a cage, and my heart is a bird beating against it to break free.

Gripping onto the fabric of his shirt, I want to tug him closer, and I'm tempted to, but before I can, he's pulling away. He breaks the kiss and presses his forehead against mine while placing his hands on either side of my head against the wall.

We're both panting and out of breath. His chest rises and falls rapidly, like kissing me was running a mile uphill.

Licking my lips, the coppery tang of blood lingers on my tongue. It's both shocking and alluring. *How can I like this? It's wrong...*

"You're everything, Dove. Everything. You have no idea the things I've done for you. The blood that's covered my hands. The darkness I've endured, but that's okay because now you're mine. You're here, and you're mine, and it was all worth it in the end."

Everything he is telling me confuses me more. Blood? Darkness? Is he telling me he's hurt people for me? I don't want to know, don't want to ask, but I know, eventually, I'll have to because deep down, I need to know.

"I'm going to put the groceries away and meet you in the bedroom. Take a shower, so we can get ready for bed."

"Bed?" I croak. That's when I remember what he said earlier when he showed me the house. He said *we'll be sharing the bedroom*. I've been so occupied with trying to escape, that I forgot about that part, or maybe I just wanted to forget it.

He wants me to sleep with him. This insane man who drugged and kidnapped me is making me sleep with him.

"Yes, bed, it's late, and you should rest since I had to give you that drug. It'll take a little while to completely wear off. Now go shower."

He puts some much-needed space between us, though it looks like it's the last thing he wants to do. In fact, he looks like he wants to ravage me, consume me, breathe me in until there's nothing left. Like watching a bad accident happen right before your eyes, you can't make yourself look away, and that's how I'm feeling right now.

When I don't move, Zane gives me a dark smirk that gets the blood pumping through my veins. "Go, now. Before I strip you bare and take what's always been mine." The muscles in his forearms tighten, and his fists clench a little tighter, and it's almost like he's holding himself back.

Always been his?

That thought gets me moving, and I scurry away from him, practically running to the bedroom. Once alone, I finally feel like I can breathe. I touch a finger to my lips where the kiss lingers and wonder why I'm feeling this way?

Something is terribly wrong with me.

12

Zane

Scrubbing a hand down my face, I ignore the raging hard-on I'm sporting between my thighs. *Fuck*, it was just a kiss, but that little touch of our lips was like a lightning bolt of pleasure zinging through me, making my entire body come alive.

My skin tingles and feels hot to the touch. I feel so incredible, I couldn't care less about my swelling face or the open cut on my cheek.

It's no surprise that she's fighting me on every corner, not that I expected anything less. That doesn't mean it doesn't bother the shit out of me though. I want her to trust me, want her to believe that I'm protecting her. That my intentions come from a good place. I mean, how can she still not see that? I guess she needs more time.

Yes, in time, she will understand. Soon enough, it will make sense to her. She will learn to trust me, see that I mean her no harm. I know she's scared and unsure, so I need to give her more time to digest everything.

This place is so quiet that I can hear the shower running through closed doors and from across the apartment. Which, of course, doesn't help my boner any. Immediately, my mind conjures up an image of Dove in the shower, naked, her skin covered in bubbles. Her delicate fingers slipping between her legs. Maybe touching her pussy at this very moment. *Shit*, this is not helping... thinking about her naked is not going to help me keep myself in check.

Looking down at my steel hard cock, I groan. Soon... *very soon*, but not today.

I make one more run upstairs to the car. When I come downstairs this time, I'm a little more careful. I wouldn't hold it against Dove if she tried to hurt me again, she's a fighter after all. She might not look like it on the outside, but she is stronger and braver than many people I've met. I doubt she's giving up so fast. She'll continue to push me, and that's not her fault. It's just not in her to give up, and I admire that about her. Her determination.

By the time I've put all the groceries and supplies away, the sound of running water has stopped, and I know she is finished with her shower. The ache in my balls has subsided a little, but having her so close, and yet so far away at the same time, makes the cravings unbearable.

Making my way back into the bedroom, I wonder if she is going to try and fight me on our sleeping arrangements. I'm sure she will. If she's trying this hard to escape, I can only imagine what she plans to do to get out of sleeping beside me.

Stepping into the room, I find her standing in front of the dresser wrapped in a fluffy white towel. The long strands of her brown hair cascade down her back while beads of water cling to her skin. I want to lick them away. Lick every inch of her body until she's completely spent and can do nothing but lay there as I take her over and over again.

Biting back a groan, I force the thought away.

"Nightgowns and Pajamas are in the second drawer, I believe," I say, making her jump a good foot off the floor as she turns around.

"I didn't hear you walk in," she whispers, staring at me with a puzzled expression as she white knuckles the towel. I wonder what she's thinking. Does she think I'm going to attack her? Rip the towel away and ravage her?

After a moment, she turns back around to face the dresser and opens the drawer, causing the thought to evaporate into the air. She pulls out a pair of flannel pajamas, and while holding onto them with a death grip, she disappears back into the bathroom. Her need for privacy is laughable. I want to tell her that there is no need to hide from me, that I've seen her naked many times over the years, but I don't think she's ready to hear that yet.

I've shared enough with her today. We have many weeks to come to discuss all of these things. While she is getting ready in the bathroom, I strip out of my clothes and slip into some sleeping pants. Usually, I sleep naked, but since I'm making a conscious effort to make Dove comfortable, I opt for clothing. She's not ready to see me naked, yet. A moment later, she reappears in the doorway. I can see her hardened nipples through the sleep shirt she's wearing and saliva pools in my mouth.

Fuck me. I used to think it was so hard to see her and only be able to watch her, but I was wrong. This is a far more difficult battle. Dropping my gaze, I take in the rest of her body. Clean, dressed, safe.

"The bathroom door doesn't lock," she says as if I didn't know that already.

"I know. None of the doors lock except the main entrance and the gym." A tense moment of silence blankets us. Pulling the covers back, I ask, "Do you need anything before we go to sleep? A drink of water?"

"I'm not sleeping with you." She lifts her chin into the air. Her defiance really is a fucking turn on, and if she didn't matter so much to me, I would snap her in two.

Turning to face her fully, I don't bother making my voice soft, there is no way she will win this fight. "You will sleep with me in this bed. This is one thing I insist on. I've waited too long for you to not sleep in the same bed with you now. So, you can either come to me on your own, or I will drag you to the bed and tie you to it. Choose, but either way, you're sleeping beside me."

Slowly she blinks as if she's not sure she heard me correctly.

"What's it going to be?" I ask, my patience slipping.

Padding over to the bed, she climbs up onto the mattress, a look of rage on her face. God, she is adorable when she's mad. She lies down at the edge of the king-sized mattress and pulls the blanket all the way up to her chin.

Her gaze stays trained on me the entire time, like I'm a big bad monster. I can see fear, anger, and curiosity swirling around in the dark depths of her ocean colored eyes. I didn't bother putting a shirt back on, and just like earlier, she stares at my bare chest when I climb into the bed, taking the spot beside her.

Her cheeks are a hue of pink, but when she realizes she's been caught, her face turns bright red.

"It's okay to look. You don't have to be shy with me."

"It's wrong. You're a monster. You kidnapped me."

Ignoring her words, I roll onto my side and pat the spot beside me. "Come here. I want to hold you."

Her lips press into a firm line, and she shakes her head. "I'm fine here."

Sighing, I reach for her, throwing an arm over her middle, I drag her toward me. "When I said sleep, I meant in my arms."

"I don't want to sleep this close to you. I want to go home." She squirms against me and rolls onto her side, facing away from me. Tightening my hold on her, I crush her back to my chest and keep her there. It takes a few minutes, but eventually, she stops struggling.

I guess it's because she feels my cock hardening and pressing against her ass while struggling. Burying my face into the back of her neck, I inhale deeply. For the first time in a very long time, calmness sweeps over me. The same calmness I felt all those years ago when Dove held my hand and told me everything was going to be okay.

Years of pain and anguish are washed away in the blink of an eye and all because I get to hold her, finally. All I feel is Dove. Her warmth surrounds me, her sweet scent tickles the hairs in my nose. And I'm reminded that this isn't a dream. This is real. The steady rhythm of my heartbeat drums in my ears and I squeeze her a little tighter.

"Goodnight, Dove," I whisper into her hair. She doesn't say anything back, but that doesn't bother me; soon enough, she will see things for what they are.

For a while, her tiny body shakes with fear, but when she realizes I'm not going to do anything, she relaxes into my arms. It doesn't take long for sleep to find me, and I hold Dove in my arms the entire night, my love for her an unbreakable prison that she will never escape.

My muscles ache when I finally open my eyes. Having Dove in my bed was both heaven and hell. Heaven because I was finally holding her, finally sleeping next to her, and hell because she woke up every few hours trying to wiggle out of my grasp. Every time she fights me and tries to get away, it's like a small stab in the heart.

"Can you please let me go?" she whispers sleepily. "I have to use the bathroom."

"Sure," I murmur into her hair before reluctantly releasing her. She climbs out of bed and disappears into the bathroom as if she can't get away fast enough. Lying on the bed, I watch the door, waiting for her to reappear. My cock has made a tent in my sleep pants, and there's no point in hiding my arousal.

When the door creaks open, and her head pops out, her eyes go straight to the tent, and those plump lips of hers part on a gasp before fear flickers in her gaze.

"There isn't anything to be scared of. I'm not going to attack you. I'll wait till you're ready. I can control myself."

She makes a choking sound. "Ready?"

I smirk. "Yes, when you're ready. I'll wait till you're begging me to fuck you, then, and only then, will I touch you."

"You'll be waiting for a long time because I won't ever beg you. I didn't even want to sleep next to you. The last thing I'm going to do is have sex with you." She turns her button nose up at me as if doing so would hurt my feelings.

All I can do is let out a harsh chuckle. "Sure, sweetheart. Whatever you say. Let's go have some breakfast and then I'll show you the library. We have plenty of time to argue, but I'd prefer to do it after I have my coffee."

Dove doesn't respond, and I toss my legs over the side of the bed and stretch my arms above my head, releasing a loud groan. Looking over my shoulder, I find Dove staring at me, when she sees me watching her, she looks down to the floor.

As amusing as it is to stand here and watch her squirm with embarrassment, I really could use some coffee. "Come, let's eat breakfast."

Dove follows behind me, her feet move with little noise. Heading straight for the coffee pot, I prepare the coffee and then get to work on breakfast. I don't bother asking Dove what she wants for breakfast. I know what she likes, what she's allergic to. Her opinion when it comes to meals isn't needed because I won't ever make her something she won't eat.

Preparing eggs and bacon for us, I place a plate down in front of her and lean against the counter, taking a gulp of the steaming hot coffee. Thankfully, Dove eats without complaint, and when she's done, I take her plate and put it in the sink.

Then I gesture for her to follow me.

As we walk down the hall, past the gym and toward the library, Dove asks, "How long will I have to stay here?"

"Until it's safe, and I'm ready to leave." I stop us directly in front of the door. Her cheeks are a soft pink, and her bee-stung lips are begging to be kissed. My attraction to her is spiraling out of control. I'm going to need to get a grasp on it.

Reaching for the door handle, I twist the knob and push the door open. I revel in the audible gasp she releases at the sight. I wasn't lying when I said I built this place with her in mind. Her love for reading was front and center when I designed the bunker. In fact, she's the only constant in my mind. The only person that matters.

Walking inside, I watch her face, the way her gaze widens, and her lips part. She's both shocked and in awe. I knew she would love this room.

Turning to me, she asks, "You built this for me?"

My heart lurches in my chest because, for the first time, she's looking at me like I'm more than her captor. Some deeper feeling swirls in her eyes, and right then, I wish she could remember me. Remember that night. Remember where it all started.

13

Dove

The rest of the day is tense. I try to keep myself busy reading and watching movies, but nothing holds my interest because my mind is too exhausted trying to make sense of my situation. I still catch myself thinking that this can't be real, that I must be asleep in my bed. That any minute now, I'm going to wake up and laugh about the crazy dream I had.

Curled up in the large recliner in the library, with Max cuddled up next to me, purring away, I do my best to focus on the book I'm reading. Looking at the pages, I read the same paragraph for the third time. *This is pointless.* Zane has left me alone for the last few hours, giving me space, he said. As if that was the issue here.

When I hear approaching footsteps, my head snaps up, and I drop the book I've been trying to read for thirty minutes into my lap.

"Would you like to work out with me?" Zane asks while leaning against the door casually.

"What... how?"

He chuckles. "In the gym. Do you want to work out? There is a stationary bike, a treadmill, and a rowing machine."

"Oh..." I'm about to decline, but then I remember that there are probably heavy weights in the gym, weights I can use as weapons. "Sure, I'll come."

Looking pleased about me taking his invitation, he nods and starts to walk away. "Come, let me show you the rest of your closet. I got you some workout clothes as well."

I've been wearing these thick pajamas all day, which are comfortable as hell, and it's not like anyone will see me here, so there really isn't a reason to change, though I guess I won't be able to wear these while working out. Getting up from the recliner, I follow him through the apartment and into the bedroom.

Pulling out the drawers, he shows me what's in each one, then he walks to the large mirror that spreads from floor to ceiling. He pushes a button—I hadn't noticed—on the side of it, and the mirror slowly swings open.

"Oh, wow," I exclaim as the enormous walk-in closet comes into view. He walks inside, and I follow behind him, too curious not to.

"This side holds all of my clothes, and these two sides hold yours. Workout attire is over there." He points to the far right of the wall.

"Wow," I repeat because, really, it's the only thing I can think to say. This whole thing is so unreal. He bought all of these things for me? People don't just spend money on other people, not unless they care about them, so why did he spend all this money on me? Why did he build this fortress and bring me here? Is it because he's obsessed with me?

I snap out of it when he grabs something from his side of the closet and starts to walk out. "I'll give you a minute so you can get dressed and meet you in the gym."

All I manage is a nod, still baffled by the number of clothes and shoes he got for me. I wish I could say that I don't care about any of this, that material things don't matter to me, but that would be a lie. The sad truth is that these things do mean something to me. They mean a lot. Growing up poor, I never had pretty clothes or even *new* clothes. I was simply glad when I got clothes that would somewhat fit me and didn't have huge holes or stains on them.

Having him buy all this stuff for me, providing me with the things I need, has my stomach in knots. I've never been so conflicted in my life.

I want to hate him. I want to feel nothing besides anger toward him, but looking at what he's done for me, has my feelings and thoughts twisted, a knife piercing me in the gut.

No, I can't let him do this to me. This was probably exactly why he did this. He's trying to buy my trust, trying to make me thankful. Thankful that I have him, thankful that he got me all these things. A sour taste fills my mouth.

I can't let him win. I need to keep a clear head. No matter what he does or says, he is the enemy, and I can't forget that because the moment I do, all chances of me getting out of here will be lost. I can't get wrapped up in this game he's playing.

Searching through the clothes, I pull out some capri pants, a sports bra, and a loose-fitting T-shirt, which I switch into quickly. Then I find a pair of socks and running shoes, which, no surprise, are my exact size. Putting those on as well, the last thing I do is put my long hair up in a ponytail with a hair tie that I find in the bathroom.

As I walk to the gym, my mind wanders. I've come to the conclusion that Zane's obsession with me knows no bounds. I wonder just exactly how much he knows about me? How long has he been stalking me, watching me? I shiver at the memory of being watched —at the fear. It was him all along, it had to be, but the biggest question is, why?

I walk into the large room, holding a plethora of fitness equipment, too many to count, but my eyes land on one in particular. It's a metal bar hanging from the ceiling.

Attached to that bar is a shirtless Zane doing pull-ups. I remember having to do them in school, hating that I was so weak I could barely do a single one. Zane makes it look like it's the easiest thing in the world. Up and down, back up and down, without stopping.

His back is turned toward me, and all I can do is watch his bulging muscles flex as he repeats the motion. I'm so mesmerized, I'm frozen in place, forgetting for a moment why I'm even here.

Suddenly Zane stops. He is just hanging from the bar now, his arms extended like he is catching his breath.

"Enjoying the show?" His deep voice fills the room. Even though he is facing the other way and can't see my face redden, I look away embarrassed. Only then, as I avert my vision to the wall, do I realize that the entire left side of the gym is a giant mirror.

Shit. He caught me watching him. Again.

A little bit flustered and more than ashamed of myself, I walk over to the treadmill and start walking. Seeing that one wall is a mirror, ruins my plan to sneakily attack him with a weight. Even if he turns away from me, he would be able to see me coming.

It's like he thought of everything.

～

AFTER SPENDING some time in the gym, Zane makes us dinner, and I do my best to ignore the way his muscles clench and work as he moves about the kitchen. I have to be sick, or this is really nothing more than a fucked-up dream. *That has to be it.*

I don't understand why I am drawn to him, why my treacherous body is attracted to him. It's probably because I've never been with a man. No one wanted me until now. Of course, leave it to me to attract the psycho kind.

"You've been very quiet today." He states as we sit down to eat.

"I'm trying to figure out why you want me. What's so special about me?"

Zane smiles, showing off his stupidly straight, white teeth. "You're special because you're mine, and that's all you need to know. I brought you here to protect you, and that's what I'm doing." He shoves a piece of broccoli into his mouth and starts chewing.

Frustration bubbles over inside of me. "You keep saying that, but it makes no sense. The only person I can think that I might need protection from is you."

Shock overtakes his features, and then his face goes blank. "There are far worse people out there than me. People that will kill and rape you. Sell you. Make you wish you were dead a million times over."

Wanting... no, *needing* to hurt him, I lash out. "And you know this how? Because you're one of them? Because you've done all those things and more?"

Zane's eyes zero in on me, and they are dark, punishing. The hand resting against the table closes into a tight fist. The veins in his arm bulge. Is he going to snap? Part of me hopes so. It's so hard when he's kind and caring, I really need him to be angry and cruel. I'd much rather have his fury, than kindness.

"I've been kind to you, Dove. I've done everything to make you feel at home and comfortable. I haven't hurt you. I haven't taken from you, and still, you make me out to be some evil villain."

"Evil? Isn't that what you are though? Isn't that what kidnapping and drugging someone is? I'm here against my will. It's wrong. Your obsession with me is wrong. All of this is wrong!" I shove out of my chair, my emotions spiraling out of control.

I don't make it two feet before Zane grabs me, spins me around, and has me pinned to the dinner table face down. He holds me in place, his fingers digging into the back of my neck. The weight of his body presses against me, and I feel his hard cock against my ass. Fear swirls deep in my belly, and I hold onto it. Fear and anger are what I need right now. I need this because I refuse to take his kindness.

"There is something wrong with you, and I refuse to think just because you haven't hurt me yet that you won't. You're no better than any other person who kidnaps and murders people," I scream and continue my struggle against him.

Snaking his other hand beneath me, I feel his fingers at the waistband of my capris. The air ceases in my lungs. This is what I wanted, right? Why I lashed out?

"Do you want me to hurt you, Dove? Do you want to see what happens when I let myself go? I can assure you it's not something you'll forget." Warm breath caresses my earlobe, and then I feel it. His tongue flicks against the sensitive flesh. I bite my bottom lip to keep the cry in. It feels so wrong.

When I don't respond, his grip tightens, and I let out a whimper. "Answer me. Is that what you want? Is my kindness not enough... do you need my anger too?"

"Let me up. I hate you. I don't want you to touch me or look at me!"

Zane chuckles darkly and cups my pussy. "That's not what I asked you, Dove." There is a hint of warning to his voice, and my body starts to tremble.

"I don't want this," I hiss, finally getting the words to come out.

"But you do... I can feel you, feel your warmth, the tiny wet spot on the front of your panties."

My breaths quicken, and my pulse races at a million miles per hour. *This is wrong. I don't want this. I don't want him.*

"You said you wouldn't hurt me."

"And I won't. I'm not hurting you right now, am I? I think I'm doing quite the opposite. I'm going to make you feel good. All you have to do is let me."

"Stop," I gasp, feeling his fingers gently graze my center. Pushing back against him, he leans in more, pushing more of his weight into me. Keeping me in place.

"Why? Isn't this what you wanted?" His voice is cruel, sinister. His finger rubs against my clit, back and forth, back and forth. His strokes are meticulous, and pleasure like I've never experienced before blooms deep in my core.

"Oh, god..."

The pleasure mounts.

It's dangerous. Unstoppable. It grips me by the throat and refuses to let go. My nails dig into the wood of the table. I need something to hold onto, something to keep me grounded.

"Come for me, let me feel how much you *don't* want this." Zane pants against my ear, and as if on command, my body does just that. Light flashes before my eyes, and I explode like a rocket. Shattering into a thousand pieces, my muscles tighten, my core clenches around nothing, and a muffled cry escapes my lips.

Tears sting my eyes because this is wrong, but it feels right.

As I drift back down to Earth, Zane gently removes his hand from my panties, and the weight of his body on mine disappears. I feel like mush, every muscle exhausted. Even though I don't want to, I push off the table and turn around just in time to see him shoving his finger in his mouth. His eyes fall closed, and dark, untamed pleasure overtakes his features.

"Lies. You taste like lies." His eyes flash with primal hunger. "Next time, don't provoke me. I told you I wouldn't hurt you, but I'm not a saint. Every man has his limits..." Before I can conjure up a response, he walks away, heading for the bathroom. The place I planned to run and hide.

14

Zane

I shouldn't have done that. Shouldn't have let myself go like that. I shouldn't have let what she said bother me, but like I knew she would, she's crawling underneath my skin. I'd prepared for this for a long time, for a time and place when she would be all mine, but like most things when it comes to Dove, I never expected for it to really happen. Her ill thoughts of me are the most frustrating part.

Yes, I've killed, outright murdered, and hurt people. I've done things that no one can fathom doing, but for her to compare me to the rest of the monsters that want to harm her... I just can't stand her thinking of me that way.

I've spent years protecting her, shielding her, making sure she had a nice place to live, and a good job. That no one hurt her. *If it wasn't for me.* Nails sink into the flesh of my palm. My nails. The pain brings me back to reality, but reality isn't any better than my mind.

Slamming my closed fist against the tile of the shower, I try to let go of some of the tension that's clinging to my bones. I need an outlet, but I don't have one.

Violence is a parasite, a vicious eater of all the good in you. It's also the only thing that keeps me from becoming a full-fledged serial killer, and since I have no one to hurt, and no one to destroy here, I'm going to need to control myself better. Which means I'm going to have to work through my emotions instead of shutting them off.

Sighing, I scrub my skin hard, drawing out the pain, reveling in it. I knew this wouldn't be easy, but I don't understand her need to provoke me. Does she want me to hurt her?

Something inside my chest squeezes. She was probably expecting the worst, and all I've given her is the opposite. I can imagine she's confused as fuck, but there isn't anything I can do to fix it. Not yet. I don't want to tell her the extent of the danger she's in yet. If I do, she'll want to know why and from who, and I don't have any of that information.

The more I think, the more pissed I get.

Fuck Christian for putting us in this situation. As soon as I get the chance, I'm putting a bullet right between his eyes. Hell, I'll do it anyway simply because he threatened Dove. Rinsing one last time, I shut the water off and open the shower door, grabbing a towel from the rack.

My cock is still rock hard, which is annoying as hell and only adding to my frustration. I should've beat off in the shower, but I was too angry, too caught up in my damn head.

Drying off, I toss the towel to the floor and walk into the bedroom naked. It's highly unlikely that Dove is going to seek me out. Not after what happened. She'll stay hidden in the library until it's time for bed.

Fucking shit. I run my fingers through my hair, tugging at the longer strands. Her body is ingrained in my mind. Every. Single. Inch. I can still feel her tight, little body beneath mine, my cock screaming for entrance. Her tiny pussy gushing against her panties.

I wish like hell that I could've peeled off those pants and plunged my finger deep inside of her. I'm sure I would've come right then and there, right in my fucking boxers like a teenager.

Jesus, I have to stop thinking about this. Control yourself, asshole.

Stomping over to the closet, I open the drawers and grab random clothes, putting them on in a hurry. I need to get a grip, need to calm down before I go back out there. Leaning against the rack of clothing, I wait a few minutes just standing and concentrating on nothing more than my breathing. When my heart rate returns to a semi-normal pace, I leave the room and walk out into the living area. Like I expected, Dove isn't anywhere in sight.

Needing to cool off a little more, I walk into the kitchen and head straight for the fridge. I knew I bought that six-pack of beer for a reason.

Grabbing one, I twist the cap off and bring the bottle to my lips. I take a long pull, letting the refreshing beer cool my heated body. It doesn't take long for me to finish the first beer, and when I'm done, I toss the bottle in the garbage and grab a second, which I drink a little slower.

Easing into the leather of the couch, I sit in silence and drink my beer. After a short while, I hear the soft patter of feet coming my way. Never one to shy away from confrontation, it's hard for me to watch as Dove stops at the entrance of the living room staring at me for a good second, big, blue eyes wide with apprehension before darting to the bedroom.

Does she really think that horrible of me? I squeeze the bottle a little tighter.

The sound of the shower turning on fills the apartment, and I force myself not to think about her naked. I've made it this long without fucking her, I think I can handle a little longer.

Finishing the last of the beer, I get up and take the bottle to the trash. Standing there, I consider the fact that Dove could easily use the bottles to try and hurt me. In fact, I wouldn't put it past her, but with my watchful eye on her, it won't happen.

She got me good with the lamp, but now I know what to watch for. When I hear the shower turn off, I start to prepare an apology in my head. I don't want her to be afraid of me, so I'll apologize and make everything better.

The apology never comes though because when I enter the bedroom, I find Dove completely naked, the towel at her feet. I'm only a little shocked, not fully since I've seen her like this before.

"Jesus Christ, have you ever heard of knocking!" She squeals, cheeks red with fury as she plucks the towel up off the floor. She wraps it around herself, but not before I catch a glimpse of her perky round breasts and pink, dusky nipples.

The towel blocks my view of her pussy, but I've seen it enough times to know that it's completely bare and most likely soft and warm, just like the rest of her.

"One, there is no privacy between us. Two, I've already seen you naked, so I don't know why you're hiding." That gets her attention, and those pretty blues widen with shock.

I watch her throat bob as she asks, "What do you mean, you've seen me naked?"

"Many times, yes." I know my confession is going to scare her, and it's not the apology I had planned, but there isn't any point in hiding my feelings from her.

"There is...there is something wrong with you. How did you watch me? When? How?" The questions tumble past her lips, and her knuckles turn white as she holds the towel with a death grip.

"Camera feed that I installed in your house. I will add it was for your protection entirely, but I did watch you. I also checked on you every night while you were sleeping."

Her body starts to tremble as more truths come out. "You... you were in my house? You had cameras?" She looks like she's going to pass out, and that's the last thing I need or want. If she falls, she could hurt her head. Taking a cautious step forward, I reach to steady her.

Fear flickers in her eyes, and she shakes her head in disbelief. Scurrying backward, she collides with the wall in her haste to get away from me.

Looking up at me with confusion and fear, she whispers, "What is wrong with you? Why would you watch me?"

I tell myself not to move. Not to corner her, but the truth is, I want to. I want to make sure she stays right where I want her. While I don't want to hurt her, I need her to understand that I will do anything, kill and hurt anyone to keep her with me.

"Because you're mine. I've told you this already and when I can tell you more, I will. I'm doing my best not to scare you. I don't want you to be afraid of me, Dove."

"Afraid?" A humorless laugh fills the room. "Afraid isn't the word I would use. I'm outraged, sick. I'm past afraid." Her words cut through me like a knife, but I remind myself that this is all new for her.

"You should get dressed so we can get ready for bed," I say, ignoring her outburst. "Unless you want to sleep naked, which I am more than fine with."

"Why do you do that?"

"Do what?" I cock my head to the side.

"Act like it's not a big deal. Like this entire thing isn't completely fucked up."

"Because it's not. Not for me. Now, are you going to get dressed, or am I going to have to dress you myself? I'm tired and done fighting with you for the night."

Dove wrinkles her nose in disgust at me. "If you touch me..."

All over again, she's taunting me. "Or what? I didn't bring you here to hurt you. I could've done that back in your apartment." The mask on my face cracks a little. "All of this is for you, now get dressed, and get in the bed before I do it for you. If you want to act like a child, then I will treat you like one."

"I'm not sleeping in that bed with you again. I'd rather sleep on the floor." Fear gives way to anger, and she walks right past me and into the closet. I go to the nightstand and pull out the handcuffs I stashed there. After what I just told her, and her reaction, I don't feel like being forced to strong-arm her all night. Handcuffing us together is the easiest solution, that way, even if she was able to hurt me, she'd have to lug my body around.

When she emerges from the closet and sees the cuffs in my hand, she pauses. Her eyes flick from the cold metal and back to my face again. Fear. That's all I see, and I know what she's thinking. That I'm going to take advantage of her, hurt her, but I'm not.

Before I can say anything, she whirls around and rushes out of the room.

Fucking Christ. She's halfway up the stairs when I enter the living room, and by the time I reach her, she's screaming and beating her fists on the door as if someone is on the other side coming to let her out.

Wrapping my arms around her, I pull her to my chest and hold her tightly even as she kicks and screams.

"You said you wouldn't hurt me. You lied! You're a liar!" She continues to struggle against my hold. Throwing her head back, she smashes it into the side of my face, barely missing my nose. Pain lances across my cheek, and I squeeze her a little tighter. The urge to shake some sense into her is strong.

"I'm not sleeping with you!"

"You're doing whatever I tell you to," I snap.

When we reach the bedroom, I'm exhausted, my face hurts, and I'm fed up with her bullshit. I drop her down onto the mattress, and she does her best to crawl away from me, but she's not fast enough. Grabbing her by the ankle, I drag her back toward me. Her hands claw against the sheets.

She flails against the mattress, trying to kick me, but I roll her over onto her back and force myself between her legs. Grabbing both hands, I press them into the mattress and move her arms so I can hold her wrists with one hand and handcuff her with the other.

Clicking the cuff into place, I release the wrist I cuffed and cuff the other one to my own wrist. The heat of her body seeps into mine. She feels perfect beneath me, even if she isn't willing to be there.

"Please, Zane! Please, let me go! Please! I won't tell anyone. I'll just go back to my apartment, and we can pretend like none of this happened." The way she says my name... I know it's out of fear, but I want to hear her say it again.

She's desperate to escape, to feel safe, but there is no safer place on this planet than right here with me. Tears pool in her eyes, threatening to fall. A tightness fills my chest cavity. I hate when she cries, and this time it's worse because I'm the reason for those tears.

Looking into her eyes, I lean forward and say my next word with firmness. "I'm never letting you go, and the sooner you come to terms with that, the better things will be."

"You can't keep me here. Someone will wonder what happened to me. I have a job and friends." I'm half tempted to tell her the job was given to her because of me and that I have her phone and can easily text her friends to let them know, but I don't. I'm done with this conversation now. Easing off of her, I put as much space between us as I can.

"Crawl underneath the covers," I order.

She tugs against the cuff instead of listening to me, and because I'm so fed up with her, I pick her up, hauling her against my chest and move us both the way I want on the mattress.

Once lying down, she tries to move away, but there is only so far she can go with us cuffed together.

"My wrist hurts."

My chest rises and falls rapidly, anger and lust pumping through my veins.

"Stop pulling, and it won't."

"I don't want to be cuffed to you."

"I don't want you to act out, but you continue to, so I guess neither of us got what we wanted. Now go to sleep, or I'll find something to gag you."

"You wouldn't." I can hear the shock in her voice, and because I'm an asshole and already pissed off, I feed right into her fears.

"I would, and worse yet, I would enjoy it."

I hear her gasp and can only imagine how red her cheeks are right now. Thankfully, that shuts her up, and soon silence falls over the room. She tugs against the cuff a few more times, trying to get comfortable but eventually stops moving.

Time passes slowly, but Dove soon falls asleep. Her even breaths giving her away.

Her body gravitates toward mine in the night as if her subconscious knows what her mind doesn't yet.

That she's forever safe, in my arms, in my bed, and in my heart.

15

Dove

I curl up into a tight ball. Trying to make myself as small as I can, wishing I could just disappear altogether. William is next to me on the mattress, his hand tightly wrapped around mine. Our door is closed, but our foster parents are fighting so loudly, it sounds like they are in our room. The walls shake when someone slams a door shut somewhere inside the house. I jump at the noise, and William holds my hand a little bit tighter as if to tell me he's here.

"It's okay, don't be scared," he whispers into the dark room. "I won't let him hurt you."

Like a warm fuzzy blanket, his words settle over me, giving me warmth and shelter, I wish I could shelter him too. I wish I could protect both of us, but we're only kids. Our foster parents are supposed to take care of us.

Heavy footfalls meet my ear. Fear trickles down my spine. Larry is coming up the stairs. Coming for us... any time he's in the room, something bad happens. My stomach tightens with worry. A moment later, the door flies open, and my worst nightmare fills the doorframe.

The light coming from the hallway is almost completely blocked out by his body, but there is a sliver of light that casts through, allowing me to see his face.

His bloodshot eyes tell me he is drunk, no surprise there. I think he's been out at the bar every day since I arrived, and when he isn't there, he's fighting with our foster mom. He sways lightly on his feet as he moves to take a step forward, an evil smile spreading across his face.

"Hey, little bird," he slurs, stepping inside the room.

I squeeze William's hand so tightly, it must hurt him, but he doesn't make a sound. He, like myself, is frozen in place, knowing what's to come.

"Come here, Dove." He motions for me to get up, but I can't move, my limbs are useless, petrified.

"No," William says, his voice stern and almost... scary. To me, anyway.

"No?" Larry, our foster father, starts laughing. "Did little Will grow some balls overnight?" He shakes his head. "I said come here, Dove. I want to spend some quality father-daughter time in the other room." He licks his lips, and my stomach churns.

"I said, no!" William growls. "You don't touch her."

"What are you gonna do about it, Willy boy?" Larry taunts. "I thought I already taught you a lesson. Obviously, I didn't beat it into your head hard enough."

Though drunk, Larry is still fast and crosses the room, coming straight for me with ease. I'm shaking so hard, all I can do is sit there and wait for the *inevitable to happen. At the last second, Will lets go of my hand, and moves to stand. He's sluggish and I know it takes a monumental amount of effort for him to move.*

Pain contorts his features, and I want to tell him, no, to stop, but my tongue is too heavy, the words lodged deep in my throat, refusing to come out.

"I said, don't touch her!" I've never seen or heard Will speak so violently, and a new sense of fear washes over me. What if Larry hurts him again? Just as the thought enters my mind, all hell breaks loose.

Larry lunges for me, but William intercepts. I know this isn't going to end well, not for me or for Will. Everything happens so fast. Fists start flying, landing with heavy thuds against skin and bone. Tears fill my eyes as screams and grunts erupt inside the room. I can't make out what belongs to who. All I can do is pray that Will is going to be okay. He has to be, he's the only thing keeping me together here.

My mind is in disarray from fear as I helplessly watch the scene unfold.

"You're as good as dead, boy," Larry yells and pulls something from his pocket. Then I see it. Something shiny, metal... the blade catches in the light.

He has a knife. Larry has a knife. My brain screams the warning at me. I act without thinking. Without fear. Jumping up, I throw my body between Larry and William. I don't care what the outcome is, all I know is I have to protect Will, protect him like he's protecting me.

The pain of the blade as it slices through my skin barely registers in my mind. I don't care about the physical pain because there are much worse pains. Like the pain I feel as I look at William. Seeing all the blood soaking his shirt. Blood... so much blood.

"Dove! Wake up..." I feel hands on me, warm, and firm. My eyes pop open, and the first thing I do is try and sit up.

"Calm down, it was just a dream, there is nothing to be scared of..." Zane's soft voice filters into my mind, but I'm still there. In that room with him.

I would do anything to bring him back. Anything for him to be alive today. I would have gladly taken his place. I should have been the one dead.

Pressing a hand to my stomach, I look down at my sweat-soaked body. I trace the scar there... *Blood. So much blood... William died, and it's all my fault.*

"There was blood, so much blood," I whisper. Tears prick my eyes, but I blink them away. The weight of the cuff on my wrist disappears, and then he's there, right in front of me, his dark eyes piercing mine, looking at me with nothing but kindness.

"Shhh, it's okay. I've got you," Zane whispers as he pulls me to his chest, wrapping his arms tightly around me. Holding the broken pieces of my soul together.

I know I shouldn't, that it's stupid and wrong, but I seek out his comfort. Needing it so badly, it hurts. I'm too weak to deny it.

He's nothing but a stranger, but he's all I have. Clutching onto his shirt, I pull him closer. I want to embed myself beneath his skin. Burying my face in his chest, I inhale deeply. Clean. He smells like soap and man, and very slowly, the dream recedes.

As I come down, floating like a leaf through the air, I'm reminded that the last time I felt this safe was with *him*... William.

It doesn't make sense. I shouldn't feel safe with this man. He's certifiably crazy, he drugged me, kidnapped me, and that's not even mentioning all the other things that he's done, but at this moment, I wouldn't want to be anywhere else.

There has to be something wrong with me if I'm seeking out the comfort of my captor.

After what seems like forever, he pulls back, his eyes travel down my body and land on the spot where my scar is hiding under my clothes. He must've seen me holding my stomach. I expect there to be a hunger, a lustful need in his gaze, but there isn't. All I find is a tenderness that makes my chest tighten.

"You're safe, Dove. You'll always be safe with me. Whatever your nightmare was about, it was only a dream. I'll always watch out for you." Something about those words tugs on me. It takes my sleepy brain a moment to let what he just said sink in.

You're safe. I'll always watch out for you...

"That night, when I walked home from the club, did you follow me?"

"I did."

"There was a guy at the party. I think he followed me—"

"The one in the plaid shirt?"

"Yeah. He was following me home, wasn't he?"

"He was, but I took care of him." I draw in a shaky breath, not knowing how to feel about what he just said. *Took care of him.* That's code for killing him. "He wanted to hurt you, Dove, and he would have if I hadn't been there."

I know he is right. That guy would have hurt me, but did he deserve to die because of it? I feel terrible, strangely not because he died, but because I feel very little remorse, even though it's partly my fault.

Lifting his hand, he softly touches my skin there. Even through the thin fabric of my sleep shirt, the gentle touch feels like an electric shock. Not one that would make you hurt, but one that wakes you up, makes you feel alive.

His fingers dance over the scar, and he touches it the same way I touch it when I'm nervous. Closing my eyes, I let my arms fall to my side and just let him touch me. I revel in the feel of his fingers on me. Enjoying the closeness without thinking about all the craziness between us.

For a moment, I just want to be happy and feel safe. He gently tucks me back into his side, his fingers never stop caressing my stomach, moving back and forth right over my marred skin.

"Go back to sleep," Zane coaxes, his voice deeper than usual. "It's still the middle of the night."

Exhaustion washes over me again as I settle deeper into the down feather pillow. My head feels heavy, just like the rest of my body. I shouldn't feel content in his arms. I shouldn't let him touch me like this, in an intimate but non-sexual way. I shouldn't... but I am. And that's how I fall back asleep. Content and happy, blissfully ignoring the danger I'm in. Tomorrow, I'll worry about what I've let happen. For now, I'm going to let my captor give me a belly rub, enjoying every second of it as I drift back into a dreamless sleep.

16

Zane

I hardly sleep for the rest of the night. Not because I'm not tired, but because I don't want this moment to end. It feels like a dream, one I'm going to wake up from any second. I hate that she had such a nightmare, but I fucking love the way she came to me. She let me calm her down, the way she opened up, letting me hold her, touch her. For the first time, it felt like she really believed that I was more than the guy who took her.

Lying there beside Dove, I watch her chest rise and fall for a long time. My gaze moves slowly as if I'm taking a picture of each part of her. Soft, pink, plump lips, tiny nose, beautiful high cheeks. The tiny freckle in the corner, near her lip. I don't want to ever forget these moments with her.

It doesn't take long for me to grow restless. I'm used to keeping busy, so I force myself out of bed, moving slowly, so I don't wake Dove. I have some stuff to check, and I'd rather do it when she's asleep, that way I don't risk another fight or more questions I don't have answers to.

Walking out to the kitchen, I close the bedroom door behind me and head to the coffee pot. I fill the coffee filter and push the brew button, listening to the machine work. A few minutes later, I take my steaming cup of hot coffee and walk to the library.

Setting my cup down, I kneel in front of the cabinet that holds my safe. I open the door and punch in the code, watching as the heavy safe door pops open. I pull out the laptop and phone and sit down in the recliner.

The laptop and phone itself are password protected, then there is another passcode that needs to be entered every time you connect to the internet. Having a connection built into the bunker was a pain in the ass but necessary. I need to know what's going on outside, after all.

First, I check the video surveillance for Dove's place, fast-forwarding over the feed. No one has been in there, which means no one has reported her missing yet, nor has Christian sent anyone else to kill her, which is good.

Checking my phone messages next, I find multiple calls and text messages from both Christian and Diego, asking when they can expect the girl. Neither one asks about Billy, so they must not have discovered his body yet, or they just haven't made the connection.

"Hey." Dove's sleepy voice fills the room. I look up to find her standing in the doorway, curiously eyeing the phone in my hand. Her hair is a wild mess, and she looks, well, sexy as hell.

"Good morning." I tuck the phone and laptop back into the safe.

Dove watches me as I finish locking up. "I didn't think a phone would work down here."

"It doesn't. Not cell service anyway. I do have internet down here; I can make calls through that connection." I say.

"Would you let me call Donna? Or Sasha? Just to let them know I'm okay." The pleading tone of her voice makes my chest constrict, but it also gives me a bargaining chip.

"How about this? Let's have breakfast first. I need to make sure you understand the rules and are willing to follow them. If I think you can, then I'll let you call Donna later."

"Really?" she says in a high-pitched voice as if she can't believe I just made that offer.

"Really." I watch as hope blossoms in her eyes.

Together, we walk back to the kitchen, where she takes a seat at the table, and I start to prepare breakfast.

"What was your dream about?" I ask, after a moment of silence.

"I don't remember..." She must be desperate to change the subject because immediately after, she says, "You know I can cook too."

"I know, but I like taking care of you." I glance over my shoulder at her just in time to catch the tiniest smile tugging at her lips.

"How old are you?"

"Twenty-three."

"I'm guessing you know how old I am?"

"Twenty-one," I say, matter of fact. Of course, I know that and much more.

"Is there anything you don't know about me?"

"I don't think so. I'm pretty sure I know more about you than you know about yourself."

"How is that even possible?" she asks, squirming in her seat.

"I've watched you. I see things that you don't. For example, you feel weak, and you think that you're scared of everything. In reality, you are brave and downright fearless."

She makes an adorable snorting sound and shakes her head. "If you think so. What about you. I know nothing about you. Is there anything you can tell me?"

"I grew up in foster care, like you," I say, just as the eggs and bacon get done cooking. I place everything on two plates and take a seat next to her.

She doesn't say anything to my foster care remark and just nods her head. She probably enjoys reminiscing about it just as much as I do.

"What else? Like what do you do for work… or did? I mean other than being a criminal? You must've had a job at one point, like a real job, right?"

"I've only had two jobs my entire life. One is killing people for the local mob—"

Her fork slips out of her hand, making a loud clanking noise as it hits the table. She jumps in her seat, scared by the sound, or maybe by what I just said.

"A-and the o-other?"

"Protecting you," I say softly. She lowers her head and sighs deeply. I can see the conflict in her eyes, even though they are downcast.

She stays quiet for the rest of the meal. Must be out of questions for the day. When we've both cleared our plates of food, I take them and deposit them in the sink.

"You know if I let you call Donna, you have to lie to her. You can't tell her where you are... not like you know where you are anyway."

She frowns. "I'm not stupid, I won't say anything. I just want to hear her voice and make sure she isn't worried about me."

"Okay, let's call her then." At my words, she perks up, shock takes over her face. She still doesn't believe me, probably thinks it's a trap, but it's not. "Well, come on."

Dove eagerly follows me into the library, where I reopen the safe and get everything out again. I set up a secure line and call the nursing home's number. When I hear it ringing, I hand her the phone.

I watch and listen closely as she talks to the nurse, then to Donna. As soon as she hears her adoptive mother's voice, a genuine smile spreads across her face. Dove is beautiful on any given day, but when she smiles, she literally takes my breath away.

Enjoying the view of Dove being happy and content, I let them talk for as long as she wants. After about twenty minutes, we hear the nurse in the background telling Donna it's time for her morning exercise. The two women say their goodbyes, and Dove hangs up the phone before handing it to me.

"Thank you."

"Anything for you." And I mean, *anything*.

∽

I LET the hot water beat down on my tired skin after my afternoon workout. Steam has filled the entire bathroom by the time I wash my hair. Watching the water drain, my mind wanders to Dove. She was different today, more open to the idea of me not being the enemy. She is still guarded, but there seems to be less resentment coming from her now.

The image of her smiling, so happy when I let her call Donna, enters my mind. I love seeing her like this... lighthearted, joyful, simply happy. I want her permanently happy, to smile all day, to smile every time she sees me, to smile every time I touch her.

Groaning, I take my hardening cock in my hand and imagine her smiling, her beautiful, plump lips are wrapped around it. She sucks hard, taking me deep into her mouth. *Fuck*. I bet her mouth feels like heaven.

A hiss of pleasure escapes my lips. I want to be inside her so badly. I don't care where or how. Mouth, pussy, ass... Doesn't matter because eventually, I'll claim all of her. For now, however, only one will do. Anything but my fucking hand.

Pumping my cock harder, I think about how warm and wet her pussy will be. How tight she'll be squeezing my dick when I take her virginity. How slow I'll take her, savoring every inch that I gain inside her.

I thrust into my hand, tightening my grip as picture after picture of the things I want to do to Dove play behind my eyes like a movie. My balls tighten, and the pleasure builds. Just when I'm about to blow a fat load onto the shower tiles, I get this weird feeling. The feeling of someone watching me. I still my hand with my cock heavy in it. My eyes flutter open and connect with a pair of big blues.

I don't know who is more shocked, her, or me. She didn't just walk in here by accident, see me and walk back out. No, she is standing in the middle of the bathroom, watching me jerk off. She walked in here, knowing I was taking a shower.

Her mouth hangs open, and her eyes are so impossibly wide, I think it must hurt to put so much strain on them. It looks like she's about to say something, her lips moving slightly, but no words come out.

I would give anything to know what's going on inside her pretty little head right now. There's only a second for me to make my decision, a second before she turns and walks away.

A good man would tell her to get out, to go into the bedroom and wait, but after this morning, and all these years of being so close but yet so far away, I'm just not strong enough to. I want her, in whatever way she'll let me have her.

Opening the glass door, steam billows out. "I see you watching me. Take your clothes off and come in here."

Fear briefly flashes over her face, but something else emerges beneath. Curiosity? Need? Want? Even if she is afraid, this other emotion must win out because she reaches for the hem of her shirt.

Her movements are slow and jerky, almost unsure as she shoves her pants down and then pulls her shirt off. She stands there before me in plain panties and a bra, and I'm so wound up I could explode at the image. *Perfection.*

"Don't be shy. I've already seen you naked." I say as she hesitates, her fingers dipping into the sides of her panties. I can see her mind working, fighting with herself. Arguing about what she wants and what she thinks is right.

Maybe she won't do it? Maybe she'll turn around and run out of the bathroom? It would be the smart thing to do. The right thing.

Her eyes stay trained to my face as she shocks the hell out of me by slowly dragging her panties down her legs before kicking them away once they reach her feet.

Next is her bra, and it takes everything inside of me not to look down at that valley between her thighs. I've dreamed about this moment. Fucked my hand so many times to the image, it should be illegal. Hell, if she knew how often I've fucked her in my mind, she would be terrified.

"I..." Her cheeks turn fifty shades of pink as she slowly walks into the shower. "This is... I don't know why I'm doing this. I don't know you. You kidnapped me. You drugged me, but..." She shakes her head almost as if she too doesn't believe it.

Shame overtakes her features and I close the door before crossing the space that separates us. I can't allow her to feel this way. To question this. We were made for each other. We're two different sides of a fractured soul.

"You're doing it because you know deep down, I'm not the monster you're making me out to be. Yes, I brought you here against your will, but have I hurt you?"

"No," she answers nervously.

"And I won't. No matter what happens or what you do, I won't hurt you. I just want to make you feel good. Do you want that? Do you want me to touch you?" Her throat bobs, and her teeth sink into her bottom lip. I won't touch her, no matter how badly my fingers itch to unless she says yes.

"I've never been naked with a man or touched a..." Her naiveté only makes her more attractive as she refuses to say the word out loud.

Leaning into her body, I watch with pleasure as she shivers, tiny goosebumps pebbling her flesh. I want to taste her, suck on her tender skin, mark her. Make her mine. Forever.

"Did you forget that I know everything there is to know about you? I know that you're a virgin, that you've never let a man touch you, let alone fuck you."

Her chest rises and falls, drawing my attention to her perky breasts.

"Will you touch me?"

"Only if you want me to," I say hoarsely, running my fingers underneath the swell of her breast. "Is that what you want? For me to touch you?"

Her voice is so soft I almost don't hear her response. "Yes."

Forcing myself to breathe slowly, I lean into her and touch my lips to hers. I kiss her lazily, drawing out each caress until she's lifting her hands and placing them against my chest. Tiny nails sink into my flesh, and I knead one breast before switching to the other.

We're both panting now, and my balls ache so badly I feel like I'm going to blow at any second. I need a release, and soon.

"I want to touch you." My lips move across her jaw and down her throat. My kisses grow hungrier as I reach her throbbing pulse.

"You are..." She says innocently.

Easing back, I chuckle. "No, I mean, here..." I trail my hand down to her abdomen and run my finger over the top of her mound.

"I don't want to have sex," she blurts out as if we were going there right now. "I'm not ready for that."

"Not sex, sweetheart, just touching. Nothing else."

She looks like she might say no but then nods her head. I can tell she's nervous, but she has nothing to be nervous about. I'll make this good for her.

"Spread your legs a little." She immediately widens her stance, and my fingers move over her skin tenderly as if she's a delicate flower. When I reach her folds, I slide a finger between them and smirk when I find her already wet for me.

Looking down at her, she's staring up at me with uncertainty.

"Relax. I won't hurt you, and if you want me to stop, I will." Fluttering my finger against her clit, I watch as her facial features do a one-eighty. There's something wild in her eyes, like a stallion that needs to be lassoed.

"You're so reactive to my touch... like you were made for me. Fuck, I want to be inside of you so bad."

"That feels..." She trails off like she can't find the word.

"Good?"

"Yes, so good." She tugs her bottom lip into her mouth, and I'm tempted to bite it just like she is, but instead, focus entirely on her pleasure. After rubbing gentle circles against her clit for a while, I move to her entrance, exhaling all the air in my lungs as I very slowly sink one digit inside of her. Heaven. Absolute fucking heaven is the only way I could describe this. Come leaks from the swollen head of my cock, and every muscle in my body tightens.

Dove clenches around my finger, and I look up into her angelic face. She's tensing up again, it's most likely nerves; still, I have to make certain.

"Am I hurting you?"

"No... I want...you." The urgency in her voice tells me she's telling the truth, plus she's drenched, soaking my fingers, she wants this.

With her pussy in my hand, I watch her face intently as I slowly pump my finger in and out of her channel, maintaining pressure against her clit.

And fuck, what I see as I watch her is what I always imagined it would be like when I touched her. Euphoric pleasure clouds her eyes. Her pupils dilate, and her mouth opens, forming a perfect O. She looks like a sex goddess.

Her arousal coats my hand, and I know she's close, so close. Curving my finger upward, I rub against the tissue at the top of her channel. At that very moment, I feel her fingers graze my cock before gripping it fully.

Holy fucking shit. I've died and gone straight to heaven. Gritting my teeth, I barely keep myself from flying off the edge with her small hand wrapped around my cock, she's stroking me slowly, her inexperience showing but I don't care.

"Come for me, sweetheart, I can feel you fluttering, building up for release. I want to feel your tightness all around me, feel you let go. Come for me..." I whisper against her lips, plunging into her a little faster, my palm slapping against her clit.

Little sex kitten noises spill from her mouth, and her nails drag across my chest, leaving behind red marks. The pain only heightens my pleasure. I'm desperate for a release, desperate to fill her with my fucking cock. But I'm beyond desperate to know what it feels like to have her fall apart. To feel her crumble in my hands.

"I'm..." She starts but doesn't finish as she slams head-first into pleasure. Her hand stops moving on my cock, and her body arches into mine as she pushes up onto her tiptoes just as her pussy starts clenching around my finger. I'm so fucking turned on, so fucking in need of release that I shatter right along with her. Lightning bolts of pleasure zing through me, heading straight into my aching balls, and like a teenager touching pussy for the first time, I come undone, ripping at the seams.

Sticky ropes of semen erupt from the head of my cock and land against Dove's thigh, marking her. Heat rips across my skin, my heart thundering in my chest, and all I can feel is her in my arms, falling apart, her pussy creaming against my hand.

After a moment, I ease out of her and smile when my eyes catch on my release that's dripping down her thigh. I'm tempted to tell her I don't usually go off that easy but decide not to. She's not experienced enough to care, and when the time for me to take her comes, I'll make sure I give her the best fucking performance ever.

"Thank you." I press a soft kiss to the crown of her forehead, waiting for us both to catch our breath.

She gives me a half-smile, her eyes heavy with post orgasm pleasure. "I didn't do anything."

Shutting off the water, I turn back toward her. "Yes, you did. You trusted me enough to let me be a part of something special, so yes, you did do something."

She shrugs. "I didn't, not really."

I help her dry off and then slip into a pair of grey sweatpants. She hurries into the closet and comes out wearing a nightgown. Her eyes are trained to the floor, almost like she's afraid to look at me. Worry knots in my gut.

She's so quiet. I don't know what I thought would happen afterward, but I didn't think she would withdraw so much. Maybe I did hurt her, and she just doesn't want to tell me. I watched her face the entire time and felt her fall apart, but maybe I had misjudged something.

I hate feeling this way when it comes to her and refuse to bite my tongue. I have to know if I did something...

"Is everything okay?" I ask when we go to lie down for bed.

She nods but doesn't make eye contact with me. "Everything is fine. I just feel... weird, like I did something wrong. Like letting you touch me was bad."

"It wasn't bad—" I start to explain but am cut off before I can finish.

"Can we just go to bed? I don't want to talk about this anymore." Desperation coats each word, and though I want to push her to explain to me what's going on in her head, there will be other times I can do that. I don't want to fight and ruin the moment we shared, so I shut off the light and crawl into bed beside her. There is a foot of space between us, which seems strange now, after how close we were in the shower.

"Goodnight, Dove," I say.

"Night," she whispers back.

It isn't long before she falls asleep, her soft snores filling the quiet room. However, like all the nights of my life, I can't sleep and instead stare at her, watching as she finds blissful sleep.

17

Dove

The days start to blend together. Time isn't a variable when there is no clock or sunlight. Each day the walls seem to close in on me a little bit more. Sleeping, reading, and eating are what my life consists of now. At least Max isn't bothered by the isolation. He's still his purring self. I, on the other hand, have cabin fever.

I do my best to stay away from Zane, but it's a lot harder than you think. Shoved into a box, I'm forced to interact with only him, a man that has me completely baffled. Being here makes me feel lonely. There is no sun, no animals, minus Max, and nothing to do. I miss my normal, boring life more and more every day. I miss talking to people, conversation. I'm longing for that human contact you can only get outside these walls. I never realized how important that is to me, the connection to other people.

I'm in a constant battle of trying to stay away from him and trying to seek him out. So far, my brain has won, and I've managed to keep my physical urges in check, but I know damn well that that's not going to last much longer.

Ever since that night in the shower, my body tingles all over whenever our eyes meet. Stupidly, I replay what we did over and over again in my mind. His thick finger entering me, owning me. The way I spiraled out of control. How he held me through the pleasure, finishing right along with me.

Repeating to myself over and over again that he's the enemy, would be easier if my body felt the same way I did. All this confusion does is give me a never-ending headache.

I still don't know why I went into the bathroom that day. It was like my mind shut down, and my body took over. I heard the shower running, and I swear I was just going to take a quick peek. Curiosity and all. I thought to myself, it would be only fair to watch him since he watched me for so long. But then I saw him jerking off in the shower, his hand wrapped around his cock. It was mesmerizing. Even after he saw me, I didn't care. There were blocks of concrete tied to my feet, stopping me from going anywhere.

Stupid. I was stupid for letting him touch me. Stupid for craving his touch. Paging through the book, I pretend to be reading while Max snuggles into my side.

I've discovered another layer of the extensiveness that is Zane's obsession with me. It's like he knows everything, and I mean everything. It's not simple things like your favorite color or food. It's what I'm allergic to, the surgeries I've had, my work hours, and therapy schedule.

He knows things that others would never notice. Like when I touch my scar...

I try not to think about the other things he knows... like my time in foster care or that *night*. I feel a sliver of triumph because no matter how much he knows, he can't know about that night. He might have read the police report, but he doesn't know what really happened because I never told a soul.

Every once in a while, he'll share something about himself, but those moments are far, and few between and none of those things are of great significance. They're mundane things, like how he loves Italian food but hates Chinese.

I don't ask him about working with the mob, mostly because I'm afraid of what he'll tell me. Then again, it probably wouldn't be a bad idea for me to think the worst of him. It would certainly make it easier for me to hate him.

I still haven't pieced the puzzle together on where I fit into things. I don't know where and how his obsession with me began. All I know is Zane is determined to keep me here and protect me from whatever evil he feels is lurking in the outside world. Because of his kindness and the feelings he has for me, my hate and fear are becoming harder and harder to maintain.

It's impossible for me to make myself hate someone who refuses to hurt me. Yes, he's my captor, but he doesn't act like it. He treats me like a lover, he's been waiting for his whole life. Like a rare piece of glass, I'm fragile to him. Beautiful. To be put on a shelf and gazed upon. I'm none of those things though. Or at least I don't want to be.

I'm hyper-aware of his presence, and I hate it. I hate that I'm drawn to him. That my nipples harden and my core burns when he's near.

Stupid, treacherous body.

I tell myself it's because I've never had a man's attention on me before and maybe that's it, or maybe it's something else. Something I don't want to admit to. The power he has over me is terrifying. It entices me. He hasn't tried to touch me since the shower, but I know he wants to.

His gaze lingers a little longer than it should, and yeah, he might be good at hiding his emotions, but he isn't that good. The way he looks at me is how I imagine a starving man looks at a steak. Like he could devour it, consume it all in one single bite.

That single thought gets the wheel in my head spinning. What if I use his obsession with me against him? He wants me, deep down, I can see it, and feel it, so what if I try to seduce him? Maybe that's how...

"Do you want to watch a movie with me?"

A high-pitched squeal leaves my lips, and I jump about a foot off the chair. My movements cause the book in my lap to fall to the floor. "Jesus!" I press a hand to my chest to stop my heart from lurching out of it. "Maybe make some noise before you appear out of thin air."

Zane smirks, showing off two dimples. I feel my insides warming already. My hormones are out of control. He's so handsome it hurts. His body's cut from stone, his features dangerous, but alluring. If I'd seen him on the street, I wouldn't just find him attractive. I'd find him salivating.

"You need to become more aware of your surroundings. I've been standing here for five minutes now, just staring at you."

It makes sense now, how easily he watched me. He's like a ghost, or ninja, or both. And apparently, I need to pay better attention. Maybe if I had, I wouldn't be here right now.

"So, is that a yes or no?"

"Uhhh." My face heats to the temperature of the sun. "Yes, sure." I've been doing anything and everything I can to keep the distance between us.

Maybe now is the time to try and implement my plan. I don't know the first thing when it comes to seducing a man, but all I can do is try. It's my only hope. Plus, Zane knows how inexperienced I am. It's not like he'll be able to notice something is up.

Like a lost puppy, I follow him out and into the living room. I plop on the couch, letting the soft cushion and oversized pillows swallow me. Watching him put on the movie, I try to come up with a plan while also trying not to look too nervous.

By the time the movie starts, and he's settled onto the couch next to me, I've come up with nothing. My anxiety builds, stacking up like Jenga blocks. One misstep and everything could come crashing down.

"Are you okay?" Zane turns, asking me in that deep gravelly voice that reaches inside of me and refuses to let go.

I nod, afraid of what might come out of my mouth if I open it. Zane gives me a half-smile and directs his attention back to the TV.

I watch him out of the corner of my eye. He looks like he's watching the movie, but he's not. He's watching me too.

I can sense it. Feel it.

There's this fluttery feeling in my chest. Like a butterfly is tirelessly beating its wings, trying to escape.

Just do it. Make the first move. It's your only way out...

Inching closer to Zane, I wonder if he can sense how nervous I am? Gah, what am I thinking? Of course, he can. Like he said, he knows me better than I know myself, which is scary as hell, by the way.

Forcing myself to keep moving, I inch closer and closer. If I stop now, I won't move anymore, so I have to keep going. Push through the fear. Scooting closer to him, I try and keep my movements subtle, but it's a lot harder than you would think.

Ignoring the heat in my cheeks and the tension in my muscles, I keep moving until we're so close I can feel his body heat radiating into my side. Zane is huge compared to me, his body dwarfing mine, and as I attempt to cuddle into his side, I become more aware of this.

I don't know why this is so hard for me. He holds me every night, this shouldn't be any different, but it is. It's a whole lot different because he doesn't give me a choice at night. He just pulls me into his chest and holds me, whether I want to or not.

This, however, is one-hundred percent my choice. I'm initiating this. Diving head-first into dark waters. It's sink or swim time.

Trying to calm my erratic heartbeat and breathing, so Zane doesn't catch on to me, I focus on the movie and ignore the wall of muscle beside me. The tension slowly eases out of me, and I lean further into Zane until my head is resting against his arm.

I wait to see if he pulls away or even objects, but his body stays glued to mine. He's probably enjoying the nearness of my body, that I'm making an effort to be close to him all on my own. As the movie plays, I find my eyes gravitating toward the apex of his thighs.

Should I do it now? Would grabbing his penis be too on point? I don't want to come across as desperate, but honestly, I am, so does it really matter? Patience isn't really my strong point, and being here has made me even antsier.

"Are you even watching the movie?" Zane asks, catching me off guard.

"Uhh..."

"You didn't have to watch it with me just so I would hold you. Movie or not, I have no problem being close to you." I hate the way his words make me feel. Like I'm precious, a gift.

Instantly, I feel bad about deceiving him like this. He might be sick and fucked up in his head, but he really has been trying to make me feel safe and comfortable, and in a lot of ways, he has. I've never felt safer, not since Will. Zane gives me comfort, he protects me, and I know even without asking, he's done things for me. Things I could never picture.

"Oh, okay," I murmur. "I still want to watch the movie," I say, even though I haven't actually paid any attention to it.

Zane lifts his arm and motions for me to come closer. I take the invitation and cuddle into his side. He lowers his arm and drapes it over my shoulders, engulfing me in his warmth. It feels nice. Right. Like I was meant to be here.

The movie plays until the end, but I couldn't really concentrate on it. I'm in too much of an argument with myself in my head, giving myself a headache.

"Ready to go to bed?" Zane asks, turning off the TV with the remote.

"Yeah, sure..." We untangle ourselves from each other and the couch. Walking together into the bedroom, my heart is going a million miles per hour. *I can do this.*

"Are you sure you're okay? You seem tense."

"I'm fine," I say. It probably sounds as unconvincing as I feel.

Once in the bedroom, I grab my pajamas and get changed in the bathroom. I purposely leave the top buttons undone, showing off a bit more skin than I usually would.

When I get back, Zane is already sprawled out on the bed. The blanket is covering his lower half, his upper body bare. His muscular chest is on full display. My mouth starts watering, and my core tightens.

Zane raises an eyebrow when he sees me trying to walk sexy as I make my way to the bed, but he doesn't say anything. I crawl under the blanket next to him, and instead of taking our normal spooning position, I turn to face him. Draping my arm over his middle, I use his chest as a pillow.

Like this, I can hear the steady rhythm of his heartbeat, and I wonder how much faster mine is beating right now. Zane reaches over to his nightstand and switches off the light, blanketing the room in darkness.

"Goodnight, Dove."

It's now or never...

"Actually," I whisper, and let my hand trail down his stomach. Swallowing down the fear, I make it to his thigh, where I graze the rod between his legs. It's thick and hard, and suddenly I don't know if I can do this. I think I'm in over my head.

"What are you doing?" Zane's voice is like a bucket of cold water. I pull my hand away like touching him is fire.

"I-I..." Is all I can manage to get out before Zane has flipped me onto my back and has climbed on top of me.

"Don't play games with me, Dove," he says, his face so close to mine that his minty breath fans over my face. His large body looms over me, caging me in, pressing me into the mattress.

It's hard to make out his features in the dark, but I don't need to see his face to know he's angry. I can feel it like a branding iron on my skin.

"I'm not." I lie... kind of.

"You want me to fuck you? I can make that happen right now. Just say the word, and I'll rip off our clothes and slide inside of you so deeply you will never forget who you belong to. Is that what you want, Dove?"

Say yes, say yes. This is what you wanted.

I can feel his growing erection between us, long and hard, nestled between our bodies. Moisture soaks my panties, and my nipples tighten, rubbing against my shirt. My body is ready, but I...

"I don't know..." *God, I'm such a chicken.*

Leaning in even closer, he whispers into the shell of my ear, "Then don't tease me."

Just as fast as he was on top of me, he is gone. I'm still breathing heavily when he gets situated next to me. Turning us, he pulls me into his chest like he always does. I close my eyes and force myself to calm down, so I can go to sleep while wondering if I just made a huge mistake or if I barely escaped one.

18

Zane

I wake up the same way I fell asleep, with a terrible feeling in my gut. This isn't my first rodeo. I've been with women many times before, and I know Dove well enough to know she's acting out of character. This isn't her. She's sweet, naive, and so incredibly innocent. Reaching for my cock isn't something she would do... not unless... she's trying to play me. In which case, that would make perfect sense.

I don't exactly know what her goal is, but it doesn't matter. Either way, she's got it in her head that she can manipulate me. Use her body as a weapon. Ha. The thought is laughable in itself. If she were any other woman, I'd have tied her up and fucked the words right out of her mouth. Found out what she was doing with little effort, hell, I could've done it last night.

A silent rage bubbles up inside of me. She's the only person I've ever shown kindness to, and this is how I'm rewarded? We've been here for days now; she must have realized by now that I only want her to be safe. I get that she was scared in the beginning, but I've proven myself over and over again. Still, she wants to try and use me? Manipulate me? Use sex against me?

She wants to play games? Fine. I'll play along. I've been nice. I've shown compassion. Maybe I need to show her what happens when you provoke a man who is crazed with need over you. Right on cue, Dove stirs next to me.

She turns in my arms, her eyes blinking open slowly. Even though I'm angry with her, I still admire her beauty. "Is it the morning already?" She asks sleepily.

At least one of us slept well last night.

"Yes, time to rise and shine." I pull away first and start to roll off the bed when I feel her hand land against my shoulder. "Yeah?" I toss over my shoulder.

Dove is looking down at the comforter with an ashamed look. I'm tempted to tell her everything is okay, but I don't have it in me. Not right now. I'm still pissed that she would try and get me to have sex with her when we both know she's not ready.

What's her motive? Does she think I'll let her go if she does?

"I'm sorry about last night. I... I don't know what I was thinking," she mumbles shamefully, and I can see two bright spots forming on her cheeks. I wounded her last night with the way I handled things, but I had to, and I'll continue to handle them this way until she gets the point because if she pushes me too far, I'll snap, and we'll both be screwed.

"It's fine. It was a mistake. Everything is good," I say. Though my brain is screaming at me that it's not. My damn cock is permanently hard, and my balls are always aching because of her. Her sweet scent surrounds me, and her body tempts me to do sinfully bad things to it.

I want her bad enough without having her throw herself at me. I don't need to be tempted any more than I am.

"You still seem mad though." She rolls her bottom lip between her teeth. "I didn't do it to make you mad."

I tense. "No, you did it to see what I would do, but next time, I can't promise you that I'll stop myself from taking you. I've spared you this far, don't make it harder than it needs to be for me. I'm only human, and I promised myself that when the time came for me to claim your virginity, I would do so as you deserved, but you make that harder every single day."

Dove gives me a shocked look. "How do you know I haven't had sex before?"

It's too early to do this, but what the fuck, why not? It's either now or in five minutes. Turning to face her so I can see her eyes fully, I say, "Because I made sure no one would get that far. You were always going to be mine."

Her mouth pops open, and her eyes widen in shock. For a moment she just stares at me, processing the information I just gave her. "W-what do you mean?"

"You're a smart girl. You know what it means." I let her draw her own conclusions.

"You scared them away?"

I shrug, deciding not to tell her that I murdered a few of them. "I mean, you could say that, yes. I made sure they didn't come back for another date. Some I even made sure they never made it to the date to begin with." Yes, I'm a fucking asshole, but nothing and no one is going to touch or taint what's mine.

Dove is pure white snow, and I wasn't going to let some fucking asshole piss all over her. The guys she went on dates with were pigs and only wanted to get between her legs. No way was I going to watch that shit go down.

"All this time, I thought there was something wrong with me..." Sadness coats her voice, but quickly her eyes turn to fire, and she shakes her head angrily. Her statement brings my own anger down a couple of pegs. "I thought they didn't want me. That I was ugly and unlovable. I thought there was something wrong with me!"

Fuck me. Shit, I didn't expect it to turn into this. The hurt in her words, it's like a knife piercing me in the chest. Reaching for her, all I want to do is comfort her, but when my fingers graze her hand, she pulls away. She's looking at me like I've ruined her life, but doesn't she see that I've only made it better?

With a tight chest, I say, "I'm sorry, Dove. I only did it to protect you. I wasn't trying to hurt you. You aren't any of those things. You're perfect."

She moves off the bed, putting too much distance between us.

"Don't lie to me! You did it because you're selfish and didn't want me to fall in love with someone else before you had the chance to kidnap me. You wanted me alone because if you can't have me, no one can? Isn't that right?"

It takes every ounce of self-restraint I have not to grab her and throw her back onto the bed. To tie her up and keep her bound to this bed with me. Yes, everything she just said is true. No one can have her, only me. Yes, I've been selfish, and yes, I wanted her to be alone in a way. I never intended for her to feel as if she was at fault though, but there isn't anything I can do about that now. Nothing of the past matters. She's mine.

Anger fills my voice when I speak. "It wouldn't have mattered if you had found someone. I would've disposed of him and took you anyway. You're mine, don't you see that?"

Dove's tiny hands form into fists, and her body vibrates with unbridled anger. I wonder if she's going to punch me, act out on her rage?

"I'm not yours! I'm a human being with feelings. Not a pet or a *thing*. I am not, nor will I ever be yours!"

As soon as the words are out of her mouth, I'm off the bed and across the room. My heart races in my chest, and I don't think. I just react. Gripping Dove by the back of the neck, I hold her in place while staring down at her. Her body starts to tremble, and I know I'm scaring, her but maybe that's what she needs. I'm tired of her being a brat. Tired of her being ungrateful for all I've done, for us, for her.

A coldness sweeps through me. How dare she say she's not mine. She has been and always will be *mine*.

"You. Are. Mine!" I growl into her face. "I've killed for you, bled for you, sacrificed everything for you. You will be whatever I want you to be."

"I never asked you to do any of that!! I never wanted this. I never wanted you!" Just like that, I snap. My patience is gone. All I feel at this moment is anger. Burning, red hot anger. My vision blurs for a fraction of a second.

I release her nape and sink my fingers into the silky strands of hair. With a fist full of hair, I tilt her head back, forcing her to see me, really see me. Her big, blue eyes fill with fear, but I'm too far gone to give a shit. I'm done. Lifting her hands, she plants them against my chest and pushes against me, but I'm a fucking mountain and don't budge, not even an inch.

"It's never been your choice and never will be. Fight me all you want. Cry. Beg. Plead." Looking down, my eyes catch on her pulse, and I lean in, licking the sensitive skin, tasting her fear. "I'll die before you're ever free of me."

"You're hurting me," Dove whimpers, struggling against my grasp. I'm tempted to shove up her nightgown and rip her panties off of her. To teach her a lesson. If I knew I could stop there, I would. But I know I wouldn't be able to. Not even as she begs me to, so I do the last thing I want. I let her go. I release my hold on her hair and take a step back.

"I hate you!" Angry pants slip from her lips, and I can feel my own rage boiling over. I need to leave this room, get away from her.

"Hate me all you want, but that doesn't change anything. You're still mine, and you're still going to be here even when the anger passes. So, hate me. It doesn't change a damn thing."

Leaving the room, I feel like I'm drowning in my own rage. When I reach the library, I close the door behind me and sit down in one of the chairs. I hold my head in my hands for a long time, trying to get my breathing and mind back on track.

Needing to think about something else, I walk over to the safe, punch in the code and pull out the computer and phone. Dealing with some shit from the outside world should help. I set everything up and then check my email and messages. There are numerous messages from Christian, and I feel all the better about my choice of kidnapping Dove with each one that I read.

Christian: Bring me the girl, and I'll spare you.

Christian: I've sent my men to find and kill both you and the girl. You're a good kid, Zane, but you don't fuck with the mob.

Christian: Where the fuck is the girl?

Christian: You're dead.

There are at least a dozen more texts just like these. Some mentioning torture and rape if I don't give both of us up. I'm not afraid though. They'll never find Dove here. Never suspect that I've hidden her. They don't know who she is to me. Just like I don't know who Dove is to Christian, but I'll figure it out. Nothing remains a secret for long in the world we live in.

Some corrupt asshole will take the money I offer him for information. It's happened before, and it will happen again. We just need to lay low for a while, and then I can reach out to some people and get the ball rolling.

I check the surveillance on Dove's apartment. I'm not shocked to find the place completely ransacked. If she could see how her apartment looks right now, she'd be devastated, or maybe she would finally believe me that she is here for her own protection.

I've rescued her from the darkness, saved her the heartbreak. She should be thanking me instead of fighting me. Thinking about what she said angers me more, and I shut my thoughts down completely.

Locking up the computer and phone, I try to think of what to do next. I haven't had breakfast or coffee yet, but I don't think my stomach could handle either. I decide to workout. I need to get rid of this tension in my muscles. I need an outlet, and the punching bag is going to be my best chance of making it through the day.

19

Dove

It takes me a long time to get my breathing under control after he leaves the room. My scalp tingles where he pulled my hair, and my insides twist with pure rage. I've never been this angry. Consumed by hate. All I can do is think of escaping. I'm not a person to him. I'm an obsession, an object. Something he owns and that he won't let anyone else touch.

God, I can't believe he did that. All the people he took from me... *Shawn*. I can't even imagine the sinister things he did to him, to them. Fear coils deep in my gut. He said I'll never be free of him. Tears fall from my eyes and cascade down my cheeks.

He did this for his own sick pleasure. He's not protecting me. He's keeping me. Locking me up. I won't be a victim. I won't let him control me. I'm going to get out of this, no matter what I have to do. Swiping at the tears, I force myself to get dressed.

It takes me forever to put my clothes on and even longer to walk out of the room, but when I do, Zane is nowhere to be found. I feel this strange tug on my heart at not seeing him, but I push the feeling away. He doesn't deserve anything from me, least of all, for me to care about him. He's a monster, a killer, and a criminal. He may not hurt me, but he's hurt others, and that's the same thing.

The living room is empty, as is the kitchen. I continue walking toward the hall that leads to the gym and library. I do my best not to make any noise, and when I reach the door to the gym, I spot Zane. He's doing push-ups on the floor, his complete attention on counting each up and down rep. I look to the free weights sitting a few feet away.

Now is your chance...

I know if I miss or don't knock him out that I'll be screwed. There is no coming back from this, but the other option is worse. It forces me to stay here with a man who is what real monsters are made of, and I can't do that. Wiping my clammy palms against the front of my yoga pants, I walk up to the weight rack and grab a fifteen-pound dumbbell. It should do the job. Nervously, I do my best not to trip or startle Zane as I edge closer to him.

You can do it. For one brief second, I contemplate putting the weight back and walking away. I'm not the type to hurt someone, and this is going to do some damage. It's going to rip me apart on the inside. I just don't see a way around it. It's him or me, and I have to save myself.

The muscles in my stomach tighten as I lift the weight above my head. Closing my eyes—because I can't look at this—I bring it down in an arch motion. Flinching when the heavy weight makes contact, and his body crashes to the floor with a thud. I lift the weight again, aiming for the back of his head, probably what I should've aimed for to begin with.

Except as I lift the weight above my head, Zane rolls over and pushes up onto his feet with lightning speed. Fear grips onto me, causing me to freeze. The dark shadow that casts on his face is terrifying. Zane might care about me, might be obsessed, but right now, all I see is a man who wants to hurt me. My lungs shrivel up, and my throat tightens. It feels like I'm suffocating, and he hasn't even touched me yet.

He's going to kill me.

"You just don't know when to quit, do you?" His lip curls with fury, and he tugs the weight out of my hand, tossing it to the floor behind him like it's nothing.

I'm going to die. I can feel it. He's looking at me with murder in his eyes, and I have nowhere to go, no way to escape him. I swallow down the scream building in my throat as he lunges for me, his nostrils flaring like a bull.

Lifting me, he tosses me over his shoulder. I land harshly, and it takes me about a half-second before I start pounding on his back and kicking my feet.

"Keep fighting me, Dove. It makes my cock hard feeling you struggle, and we both know how badly you want me."

"Let me go! I hate you. I hate you, and I will never let you touch me again. Never." I'm screaming the words now, my voice cracking from fear and anger.

Before I can grasp onto my bearings, Zane is doing just that, letting me go, but my relief is short-lived when I'm tossed onto the mattress like a rag doll.

His firm body blankets mine in an instant, and I try to move away, but he holds me in place, his fingers digging into the flesh at my hip. "You want me to treat you the way I treat everyone else? You don't want my kindness? Because that's all I've given you so far. You still fight me and try to escape. I'm doing all of this to protect you, but you don't see that. You don't see that the biggest monster isn't me but someone else. Why can't you see the truth?"

Like a wounded animal in the clutches of a predator, I twist my body and kick my legs, hoping to land a jab against him. Zane is skilled though and stops my assaults before they can even get started by pressing me deeper into the mattress.

My breaths are coming out in pants, and it's almost like I'm suffocating. Choking on the fear. The weight of his body is all I can feel. His hard cock is against my stomach, and I think I'm going to be sick. Bile rises in my throat.

Fight. Fight! Digging deep inside myself, I lash out. I catch him right across the face with my hand and drag my nails down across his nose and cheek, leaving deep gouges.

"Fuck!" He takes both of my wrists into one hand and pressing them to my chest. Once he has me trapped, I can hardly move, let alone breathe. When he leans into my face, all I see is the devil looking down at me.

The look in his eyes is pure violence. It promises pain, suffering, agony. This isn't the Zane I've come to know. This is the obsessed man who kills without thought, who will do anything to keep me where he wants me.

"You really shouldn't have done that, Dove."

No. This isn't happening. All of a sudden, this has gotten real. His body against mine. His rock hard cock. The searing heat bubbling between our two bodies. Hate and lust mingle together.

"Please. You don't have to do this. I'm sorry..."

"Oh, I do... I have to teach you a lesson. I need to show you what you don't want to admit. We belong together, and it's time I prove it to you."

He let's go of my wrists and starts ripping off my clothes. Fabric tears and cool air kisses my skin as my bra and shirt are ripped from my body. I'm trembling with fear, but still try to shove against his chest as hard as I can to escape. There is no point though. I can't move him. He's a steel wall, cold and impenetrable.

Snatching my wrists once more, he pins them above my head this time. With his free hand, he reaches into the drawer beside the bed and pulls out the handcuffs he used on me before. A moment later, the cool metal is fastened around my wrist, and the other end fastened to the headboard. He pulls out another pair and does the same to the other hand.

"Please..." I whimper, but even I know that the time for begging has passed. I've dug my own grave, and now I'm going to have to lie in it. "You said you would never hurt me!"

"Shut up," Zane growls as he makes quick work of my pants, pulling them down right along with my panties, leaving me completely bare to him. "You've tried to kill me. How the hell do you think you would have gotten out of here without me? You don't have the code for the door. You would have died in here!"

My whole body is shaking, my fear only intensifying as he strips out of his clothes. His very hard, very angry cock comes into view, and my fear reaches new heights. It's so big, the veins bulging out on it, visibly throbbing.

I didn't think that I would lose my virginity in such a savage way, taken from me without mercy, but there isn't anything I can do to stop him.

"Is this what you wanted?" He stares down at me. "Did you want me so angry that I take from you? That I take the choice from you, so you don't have to admit that you want this?"

"I hate you," I lie. I should, but I can't, even now. I squeeze my eyes shut and try to shut the world out.

"You try to hate me, but we both know you truly don't. You can't, we are too connected, whether you like it or not. We belong together, and I'm about to show you how much." His lips brush against mine, and I move against him on instinct, seeking out his comfort even with the threat of him hurting me.

"Open your eyes and look at me as I take you. Feel every inch of my cock as I sink deep inside you." The head of his cock brushes against my entrance, and I freeze, my entire body shutting down. I tell myself to stop feeling. Tears escape my eyes and slide down the sides of my cheeks. I can't breathe. I can't swallow. I feel cold all over, broken and scared, so scared. He's going to hurt me after he told me he wouldn't, he's going to. I don't understand why that matters so much at the moment. His words don't mean shit, not after what he's done to me, but deep down, I know that's a lie.

They mean everything...

A pained cry fills the room. It takes a moment to realize that it came from me. I made that sound. Zane's body freezes above mine, but I still don't open my eyes. I can't. I do want this, but not like this. I don't want to be a victim of his rage and anger.

I try to suck in a breath, but my chest is too tight, panic holding it prisoner like a hundred-pound weight. I feel like I'm suffocating, gasping for oxygen. My mind races at the things he's going to do to me, the savage way he's going to claim me over and over again.

"Shhh." I feel the warmth of his hand against my cold cheek. He cups it gently, swiping at the tears that still linger there. It's like he knows I need this. I know I shouldn't, that I should hate him, tell him to release me, but instead of doing those things, I seek comfort in his touch, nuzzling my face into his palm, needing it. Needing him.

"I never want to hurt you, Dove. But dammit... the way you act, it makes me want to break you down just so I can build you up again. To prove to you that you need me. But I'm not sure I could come back from that. I can't see my Dove broken in her cage. I want her to sing and fly, but I'm tired of her trying to escape."

"I can't accept this..." I whimper.

"You have to, and after today, you won't be able to fly away from me, Dove. I'm going to shackle you to me. Make you mine forever. Do you understand?"

"Zane, please..." I whimper, my breathing slowly returning to a normal pace. When I finally force my eyes open, I find Zane hovering above me. There's a softness in his eyes. I want to reach out and grab it, wrap myself up in it.

He's watching me cautiously, tenderly almost, penetrating my soul with his gaze. Before, when I looked at him, there was nothing. An empty pit of nothingness. Now, there is light in his eyes, pieces of him shine through and down at me.

A rough hand skims down the side of my body, gently stroking the tense flesh. It feels like he's taking the fear he gave me and replacing it with something else, something deeper. Leaning forward, he presses an open-mouthed kiss to my breast, his tongue sliding over the flesh makes me shiver. Every hair on my body awakens at his touch. Reaching my nipple, he takes it into his mouth, flicking the bud with his tongue.

A spark of pleasure ignites in my belly, and I have to stop myself from arching into his mouth. He sucks deeply, tugging on the hard bud before releasing it with a pop. He works the other one over in the same fashion, and I feel my arousal for him dripping down my thighs. I'm drenched, my core clenching, silently begging him to take me.

I want him. Even though I shouldn't. Even though it's wrong. I still want him, and I can't deny that. I can't lie about the strange connection we have. Nothing about Zane is normal, and after all the things he's told me, I know I should be fighting him, but I'm tired of pushing him away. I want this... need it.

"I want you, Dove, and I'm going to have you. I'm going to take what's mine, own you, seal our bodies together as one. You were meant to be mine, and it's time I claim you. Time, I make you mine so no one else can."

Every muscle in my body tenses, and I think he's going to spread me wide and plunge deep inside, but he shocks me when he moves back and peers down between my legs. Dropping down to his belly, he slides his hands under my ass and lifts me to his face. He inhales deeply, and my cheeks burn. He isn't doing what I think he is, is he?

I tug against the cuffs and try to look down at him, but in this position, I'm at his mercy. Just like he wants, needs. *Dove trapped in her golden cage.*

"You smell divine, perfect, and I can't wait to fucking taste you. I've envisioned this moment for years. Tongue fucking you. Tasting your release as you explode into my mouth." His lips trail the inside of my thigh. My muscles jump underneath the scrape of his tongue. Every touch is heightened. Hot breath fans against my entrance, and I'm not sure if I should beg him to stop or keep going. Zane doesn't give me a chance to dwell on the thought long before making the choice for me.

His lips close around the bundle of nerves hidden between my folds, and the pleasure that sparks is so intense I lift my hips and gasp his name at the same time. Strong fingers dig into my thighs as he spreads me wider, his hulking frame fitting between them as if he was always made to be there. He feasts on me without care, driven by primal need. His mouth is relentless, and all I feel is him owning me, worshipping me.

I grow wetter and wetter as he sucks, and when his tongue flicks over the bud, I explode. He rips the orgasm right out of me. I'm almost ashamed at how fast I fall apart, but my brain is too drunk on lust to think about that for long. Not when my entire body feels like it's gone to heaven. My toes curl into the mattress, and I lift my hips arching into his face.

Zane presses a kiss to my mound, and then I feel a finger at my entrance. I've barely come down from my high when he slowly slides into me and starts fucking me with that single digit. All I can do is focus on the pleasure he gives me, and when my body starts to coil tight, gearing up for a second release, he adds another finger, stretching me.

I'm consumed by him, and when I look up, our eyes connect. "Come for me, fall apart so I can fuck you the way you should be fucked. Like only I can."

The intensity in his eyes, the love and want that pours out of him. He's obsessed, but his feelings are deeper than that, and I feel that now. Feel his attraction. It's like sticking your finger into a light socket.

Scissoring the two fingers inside of me, he touches that sweet spot at the back of my channel that he touched before and I come undone. Split down the middle. My muscles tense, and like a rubber band, my body snaps. Pleasure pools in my core, and I clench down on his fingers, my channel gripping him like it never wants to let go.

"Tell me you want me... that you want my cock," Zane says as he eases his fingers out of me. My gaze flicks down to his massive cock.

Come beads the tip as it bobs in the space between us. Can I do this? Take him? I'm afraid... but also spellbound with need.

I want him, need him.

"Yes, take me..."

The words have barely left my lips, and he's on me, centering himself between my legs. Hovering above me, his entire body vibrates. He's so big and warm, and I feel safe. I feel safe in my captor's arms. Snaking a hand between our bodies, he guides the crown of his cock to my entrance, and I tense. I look up at him and find him watching me.

"There is no way around this. It's going to hurt, but I promise I'll be as gentle as I can," he whispers hoarsely, and relief floods my veins.

He won't hurt me. He won't just take.

I try and relax as the head of his cock enters me, but I can't. It feels like he's taking everything from me. Pain. Pleasure. Love. Hate. My lungs tighten, and my thoughts become dizzy. It's like he's ripping me in two.

"Breathe, baby, breathe for me." Zane sounds as pained as I feel, and I realize I'm not breathing then. Sucking in a shaky breath, I half expect him to just plow into me at that moment, but he doesn't. He takes his time, savoring every inch he gains. Pain ripples through me, overtaking the pleasure.

I feel full, so full, and when he reaches the resistance of my virginity, he smiles. He actually smiles as he thrusts forward and claims it. Like a prize that can never be returned or given to another, he makes certain I will always remember him. Remember this moment. No matter what happens, I will always know who my first was.

Peppering my face with kisses, he thrust a little deeper, and I whimper when his balls press against my ass. He's all the way in... he's inside of me. His muscles strain, and a bead of sweat slides down the side of his face.

His lips find my ear, and he stills inside of me. I can't imagine the amount of self-control it's taking for him not to plunge into me over and over again.

"Fucking Christ, I can't tell you how many nights I fucked my hand thinking about your pussy. Imagining how warm and tight it would be. How it would feel to claim that one piece of you that no one else ever could again. Through all the dreaming, I never could have imagined it would feel this good. That it would be this perfect. That we would fit together so well, like two pieces of a puzzle." All I can do is whimper as I try and adjust to his cock inside of me.

His lips sear mine hungrily, and pleasure starts to build again when he moves a hand between our sweaty bodies and finds my clit. He strokes me gently, circling my bundle of nerves, playing them like an instrument until my entire body loosens, slowly becoming a melty pile of mush. When I start to lift my hips and mewl against his mouth, he pulls out and thrusts back in. His strokes are slow and precise at first, and though there is a bite of pain with each push, it's far more bearable with his finger on my clit.

"Am I hurting you?" he asks, our foreheads touching.

"No..." I gasp and arch into him, the cuffs around my wrists dig into my skin as he swivels his hips, touching something inside me. It's foreign, but it feels like heaven.

"Good. I want you to come with me."

"I don't know if I can... girls don't come their first time," I whisper.

Zane smiles. "Girls that are with guys who don't care about their pleasure don't come their first time. You're going to come, or I'll continue fucking you until you do."

The intense look in his eyes tells me he's not lying, and I become hypnotized by him as he starts fucking me, sinking deep into my flesh, taking and taking until there is nothing left. Until I'm a shell, and he is the harbor for all my happiness and misery.

Together we crest the hill of pleasure, me crashing into the wall and shattering first, forcing the orgasm right out of him. He fills me with his come, the hot ropes paint my womb, and since I'm riding the waves of pleasure, it takes me a moment to realize what we just did.

"We didn't use a condom." The words come out shaky as I interrupt the moment.

Zane lets out a harsh breath as he gently pulls out of me and undoes the cuffs. "It's okay. I'm clean, and you're on the shot."

I'm about to ask how he knows that, but I already know the answer, he knows everything. Zane takes my wrists, inspecting them for injury most likely. Once satisfied, he rubs the life back into my arms and then settles into the spot beside me. I can already feel the soreness between my legs, it feels like a dull ache hanging low in my belly. My gaze darts to his cock, which is already growing hard again. It's smeared with blood, my blood, and it makes me sick.

I gave myself to him.

"I love you, Dove," he whispers as he tugs me into his side, rubbing small circles against the small of my back. I don't say anything because there isn't anything to say. I don't love Zane. I can't allow myself to. He kidnapped me, took everything away from me, he stole my life.

I might feel safe in his arms, but he's not William. He's not going to save me. He's going to trap me and keep me forever.

20

Zane

Two days have passed since I made her mine completely and took that sweet cherry between her thighs. It's been a tense forty-eight hours. Even though fucking her was heaven, I didn't let it slip from my mind what she did before that. She submitted to me during sex beautifully, but she also tried to kill me. I hope she doesn't think I've forgotten that.

I've been keeping my distance, not because of her attacking me, but because now that I've had her, I can barely keep a leash on my inner beast. I want her again, and this time, I refuse to be gentle.

I always thought that once I had her, my obsessive need for her would be curbed. I knew it would never be gone, but I had hoped it would at least take off the edge.

Boy, was I wrong... so wrong.

Having her only intensified my cravings, the need to possess her is stronger now than it ever was. I want to own her in every way. Claim every hole on her body, every sliver of her soul. I want it all, and in return, I will give her the same. I'll give her the good, the bad, the angel, and the demon. I can't hide the dark side of me anymore. It's out for blood, and it wants Dove just as badly as I do.

"Are you hungry?" My question causing her to jump off the recliner. She still has no awareness of her surroundings. She never hears me coming, and always gets scared. I shake my head at her inability to protect herself. How could she ever think that she doesn't need me? She'd be dead in ten minutes without me.

"Yes, I'm starving, actually." The smile she gives me, though shy, is enough to make me want to bend her over the dining room table and fuck her senseless. She's under my skin, in my head, pumping through my body. She consumes me.

Reheating the leftovers from last night, I set two plates on the table and take the seat next to her.

"You've been avoiding me," she says in between bites.

"Yes," I admit. No reason to lie.

"Did I do something wrong? I mean... it was my first time. I'm not sure if it was okay for you." I almost drop my fork at her words.

"Do you seriously think I've been avoiding you because I didn't enjoy the sex?"

"Yeah. No. Maybe. I-I just didn't know," she stutters, her cheeks turning pink.

It would be easier to avoid her if the sex was bad, but it wasn't even close to bad.

"Maybe I've been avoiding you because you tried to kill me?"

Her face falls, and I can see the guilt written all over it. She stares down at the broccoli on her plate like it has all the answers. "I'm sorry about that," she whispers, still not looking at me. Her apology means the world to me, but it doesn't change what happened. She was so desperate to get away that she was prepared to kill me. I just can't forget that.

"I know you are, but that's not actually the reason I've been staying away."

She finally glances up at me, curiosity flickering across her face. "Why then?"

Did I want to tell her why? I could lie, but that wouldn't make any sense. I didn't want there to be lies between us. Clearing my throat, I answer honestly. "Because I knew you would be sore, and every time I'm close to you, all I can think about is stripping you naked and shoving my cock into your tight cunt."

At my crude usage of words, her mouth pops open, and the hand she is holding the fork with starts to visibly shake. *Is she scared? Aroused?*

She looks up at me through her thick lashes. "I'm not sore anymore..."

I raise an eyebrow at her. Who is she trying to convince, herself or me? "Is that an invitation, Dove? Do you want me to fuck you again? Because I'm telling you right now, I was gentle with you before because it was your first time, but this time, I won't hold back. I want you too much. I've gotta have you hard and fast."

She swallows so hard I can hear it as well as see her throat work. She puts the fork down on the table next to her plate. Licking her lips, she looks around the room, clearly trying to think of a response. When she still can't seem to find the words, I clarify.

"I want to go back to the bedroom, strip you bare, and tie you up. Not because you've done anything wrong, but because I simply like having you restrained. I like being in control, and I like you being helpless and at my mercy. I want you to submit to me, to trust that I will take care of you. I want to put a blindfold on you this time, and then I want to use your body however I see fit. Do you want that?"

Another moment of silence stretches out between us before she finally has the courage to nod. That's not good enough though. I need her to tell me this is what she wants.

"Use your words, Dove." The words come out a little more sternly than I intended, but when it comes to her, I lack self-control.

"I want you to do that," she says, finally looking up at me.

"Finish eating then." I adjust my hardening cock under the table and watch as she shoves a few more pieces of food into her mouth before she gets up and dumps her plate in the sink. I don't even bother with my plate. I just take her hand and pull her into the bedroom.

"Strip!" I order while undressing myself. Dove does as I say and gets naked, surprising me with her eagerness. She has no idea what I'm about to do to her. Hell, I don't even know how far I'll go. All I know is that I have to have her. I have to make her mine, feel our bodies pressed against each other.

Once she's completely naked, she stands in the center of the room, looking at me like she's waiting for me to tell her what to do next. I won't lie, it turns me on so fucking badly that she takes my commands.

"Get on the bed," I say and watch as she climbs onto the king-sized mattress, my eyes going straight to the valley between her legs. "Lie on your back, legs spread."

A moment later, she's spread out on the bed for me like a fucking offering. Her dark hair fanning out like a halo on the pillow, her smooth, creamy skin pebbled with goosebumps, her chest rising and falling rapidly. My eyes travel down her body and land between her thighs, where her pinks pussy lips are already glistening with arousal. Fuck, she is so perfect. I don't want to break her, but I will bend her.

"Don't move." I rush into the closet and open the bottom drawer on my side. I briefly scan over its content before choosing four items. As soon as I walk back into the room, I order her to close her eyes.

Dumping the things from the drawer onto the bed, I grab the blindfold first, securing it around her eyes. Then I take the rope and start looping it around the bed frame so I can tie every one of her limbs to it. She doesn't say a word while I tie her up, and her trust in me is the most potent aphrodisiac of all. I want her to know she's always safe with me, in the bedroom, and outside of it.

Next, I take the small bottle of lube, flip the cap open, and pour some out onto my palm. Then I bring my hand between her legs. Dove sucks in a sharp breath when my fingers find her center. Gently, I rub the lube all over her pussy, down her slit, and over her tight puckered asshole. The next virgin hole I plan to claim on her.

"What are you doing?" She gasps, half tensing as I dip the tip of my pinky finger inside her ass.

"I warned you that I was going to use your body however I wanted. Every part of you is mine. This part too," I say, pushing my finger a little deeper into her ass. A groan ripples through my chest as her muscles squeeze down on my finger. "Just relax... and trust me. I'll never hurt you. Never." I remind her.

Sliding my finger in and out, I let her adjust to the size and angle before I add a second. I know it stings and probably feels foreign, but what I'm going to do is give her the best orgasm she's ever had in her life. Stretching her tight little hole, I move my fingers faster while pressing my thumb against her swollen clit at the same time.

"Oh, god..." She cries out, and I know she's close to coming, her tight, little body trembles, and her nipples become diamond hard peaks.

Using my other hand, I grab the fourth item I brought, and pour some more lube over the small-sized butt plug, making sure it's slick all around before I bring it to her ass. Easing my fingers out, I replace them with the plug.

Dove lets out a soft whimper but doesn't ask me to stop. Thank fuck, 'cause I'm not sure I could even if I wanted to.

I take in my handy work, a smile pulling at my lips when I see her tight little asshole clenching around the butt plug. Fuck, I can't wait to be inside of her. I need her now. Right now.

"Are you ready for my cock, Dove?"

"Yes," she says, almost breathlessly.

Lifting a hand, I caress her body, letting her know where I am. Having her at my mercy is doing insane things to my head. "Remember what I told you. I won't be gentle this time. I want to fuck you raw. To fuck you until you can barely walk. I want you to still feel me inside of you every time you move tomorrow."

"Mhhm..." Apparently, we are past words now.

Gripping my cock, I give it a few good pumps before I move between her legs. I lower myself until I just hover inches over her. Her hardened nipples are grazing against my chest with every breath she takes. I line myself up with the center, bringing the tip of my cock to her entrance.

I enter her in one deep thrust, bottoming out until my balls are flush against her stuffed asshole. Her whole body arches off the bed, and the room fills with the sound of her pleasured cry. The plug making her pussy even tighter, and all my restraint is gone.

Plunging into her over and over again, I fuck her hard and fast. I go so deep, I can feel the end of her channel, the head of my cock bumping into it with each thrust.

"Do you feel that?" I ask, my voice coming out rough and gravelly. "Do you feel me deep inside of you?"

"Yes... so deep," she whimpers in between thrusts. Her head is tipped back into the pillow, her slender neck exposed to me.

"Who do you belong to? Tell me, Dove."

"You... you, I belong to you."

Like a crazed animal, I rut into her, grunting on every thrust. She moans and squirms beneath me, her small body smothered by my larger one.

Sweat forms on my skin and my muscles ache, but I can't get enough. I never want to stop fucking her like this. Raw, primal, animalistic. Hard and rough.

Her orgasm slams into her out of nowhere, her pussy squeezing me so tightly. Her thighs quiver, and a silent scream forms on her lips. Her whole body tightens before relaxing back into the mattress. My cock's harder than steel, and I'm ready to fuck her next virgin hole.

"Is your ass ready for my cock?" I ask, and she moans in response.

I pull out of her, listening to her whimper at the loss. "Don't worry, I'll be back inside of you in no time."

Making quick work of the ropes on her ankles, I untie them and flip her over, leaving her wrists tied to the headboard. Her chest is pressed flat against the mattress, her cheek pressed to the pillow, her ass hanging high up in the air. Her pink pussy glistens with her juices, and I'm tempted to taste her, to lick every drop, but there's something else I want more right now.

Moving to her ass, I carefully remove the butt plug. Her ass is still tight when I push my finger inside, but it has loosened up tremendously.

Fuck, I can't wait.

Removing my finger, I replace it with the crown of my cock. I run my hands up and down her silky-smooth skin a couple of times before I start to push inside.

Dove whimpers into the mattress. "You're too big..."

"Shhh, it's going to be a tight fit, but you were made for me. Made to take my cock in every hole." I snake a hand beneath her body and gently stroke her clit. When I feel her greedy pussy getting wetter, I push into her, watching with glee as her ass swallows my dick beautifully.

She was made for me. Made to take me in every hole. Made to be worshipped and protected by me. Mine. All fucking mine.

"Fuck, Dove... you should see how well your ass takes me. Can you feel it? How your greedy ass is swallowing me... begging me for more? You like this, don't you? Like me filling your ass? Giving yourself over to me."

"Yes... Yes... God, yes," she chants into the pillow.

I thrust into her ass slowly for a couple strokes. I'm big, and I don't want to tear her, but once I know she's stretched out enough for me, I start fucking her in earnest. I pump my iron rod in and out of her just as furiously as I was fucking her pussy moments ago.

My hands dig into her hips, and I know there will be bruises. I can't be gentle with her. I need her, every fucking inch. Each thrust is rougher than the last, and the headboard makes a loud thudding against the wall as I fuck her.

My balls are so full and ready to explode. The tingle on the base of my spine tells me I'm about to come. I pick up my speed, slamming into her as fast and deep as I can. Moans, grunts, and the sound of naked flesh slapping against each other fill the room. I'm surrounded by her scent and the sweet combination of sweat and her pussy.

"Come again, Dove. Come for me as I fuck your ass hard. Squeeze my cock."

When I feel her ass clamping down on me and her release coming, I allow myself to fall over the edge with her. My orgasm is like a tidal wave, slamming into me and flooding my body with pure ecstasy. The entire contents of my balls explode into her tight little ass, ropes of sticky come filling up her no longer virgin hole.

And I keep coming, my cock filling her ass with come. My vision goes blurry, and I feel light-headed. *Fuck. Me.*

We both collapse on the bed, and it takes a moment for my muscles to start working properly again. Dove falls asleep almost immediately. Her body is worn out from the intense sex we just had. It's done the opposite to me though. I'm like an addict who just took a hit. I'm wide awake and too wound up to keep my eyes shut.

Walking into the bathroom, I grab a rag and soak it in luke-warm water. Then I clean between her thighs, remove the blindfold and untie her wrists. I cover her naked body with the blanket and tuck her in. I press a kiss to her clammy forehead before making my way to the library. Since I can't sleep, I might as well check what's going on in the outside world.

Not bothering with clothes, I walk naked through the apartment and into the library. I get out the laptop and phone from the safe and turn on both.

As expected, there are multiple calls and messages from the Sergio family. Christian has put out an official hit on me. Ten thousand for whoever brings him my head. *Cheap bastard.* Doesn't surprise me that he wouldn't put a bigger hit out. In fact, I'm a little offended.

I'm relieved to find that he didn't put out an official hit on Dove, which is interesting.

He wants her dead, but he doesn't want people to know. That reminds me of something... he wanted me to take out people from the Castro family quietly too.

Could there be a connection?

Before I can dwell on that thought for too long, another message catches my eye. It's from the nursing home Donna is at. Immediately, I get a bad feeling. I've been paying her bills because the only place she could afford was a piss poor nursing facility, and I knew there was no way Dove would allow that, nor would I. So, I took on the cost and made up some insurance program so Dove wouldn't know. The nursing home has my number, but I told them to only contact me if something was wrong.

Hitting play, I listen to the message.

"*Hello, Mr. Brennan, this is Julie from the Westfield nursing home. You wanted us to call you if something happened to Mrs. Miller. I'm afraid to say she had a stroke this morning. She was rushed to the hospital and is currently in critical condition. Last I heard, she was in the ICU. I'm sure the hospital can give you more information. I'm sorry I had to do this over the phone...*"

I end the recording, I've heard enough. My stomach twists, and my heart rate skyrockets. Resisting the urge to throw the damn phone across the room, I close the laptop and lock everything up.

Fuck, fuck, fuck...

What am I supposed to do now? There's a hit out on my head. Dove is still in huge danger. We can't leave the safety of the bunker... but if I don't let her go and Donna dies. Fuck, if she dies and Dove doesn't get to say goodbye, she'll hate me forever.

21

Dove

I know something is wrong before I even open my eyes. It's just a feeling lingering in the air. A feeling that something bad is going to happen. Moving my hands to Zane's side of the mattress, I find the spot empty and cold. Zane isn't next to me. My heart clenches a little, and I blink my eyes open and sit up, looking around the room.

The room is dark, the only light source coming from the bathroom. The door to it is only cracked, not letting a whole lot of light in. I almost don't see him. Zane is sitting on the edge of the bed, his elbows resting on his knees, his head in his hands like he's defeated. I know instantly that something is wrong.

"What's wrong?" I ask, my voice still wrapped up in sleep. I throw the blanket off my body and crawl over to him. As he promised, I feel an ache between my legs with every move I make, a reminder of what we did last night.

Placing my hand on his shoulder, I ask again, this time a little more urgently. "Zane, what's wrong?"

He raises his hand and places it on top of mine before he starts talking. I look down at it. The gesture so gentle and kind it's a stark reminder that he can be both kind and possessive.

"I'm sorry, Dove. I have some bad news for you." The way he's looking at me almost shatters me. He takes a deep breath like he's afraid to tell me. The guy who kills people for a living, who stalked and kidnapped me is afraid? Whatever he has to say is going to be bad, but I have to know. I have to.

"Please, tell me!" My voice comes out more demanding than I wanted it to, but I can't help it. I need to know what's wrong.

Zane sighs, his eyes filling with panic. "It's Donna... she's had a stroke, Dove."

I hear the words right away, but it's almost like they don't make it further than my ear. Somehow, my brain doesn't understand them. *What happened?* The information sinks in slowly, and seconds pass before my brain can comprehend what he is telling me, but once it does, dread consumes me.

"Donna? Donna had a stroke?" I ask as if I didn't hear him the first time. He nods, and I try to ask my next question. "Is she..."

"She is alive, but she's not doing well. The nursing home said she's in critical condition—"

"I need to see her!" I cut him off mid-sentence. "Zane, you need to let me go." I tug on his arm.

"I know… but I need to make preparations. I need to make sure it's safe for you."

"Safe for me? I don't give a shit about *my* safety. The only parent I ever had is in the hospital dying, and I need to be there! Right now!" Please let him see how important this is to me because if he doesn't… if he doesn't take me to her. "Zane, if she dies and I'm not there, I will never forgive you."

He suddenly jumps up from the bed, his large body looming over me. "You think I don't know that! You might hate me forever, but at least you'll be alive! At least I won't have to worry that someone took you from me!"

"I don't care about me," I yell back at him, my face flush. I don't care what happens to me, so long as I get to see Donna before she dies.

"I know that too, but I care. I care. Do you still not get it? You're everything to me. If something happened to you, I'd kill myself. You are the only person that matters to me, and if you die, I die with you."

Tears fill my eyes, and my lungs burn. "Zane, I have to see her. I know that I'm the most important person to you, but Donna is important to me, and she's dying right now. I need to be there with her. I need to say goodbye."

His jaw turns to steel, and he lets out a growl that's more animal than human. "Fuck, Dove, if something happens to you. They're looking for you. For both of us. I can't protect you out there. I can't make sure nothing happens to you out there." For the first time ever, I see panic fill his eyes. I see fear, real fear, and it sinks in just how much I mean to him.

I thought it was just an obsession, but it's clear it's more, deeper.

"You have to let me do this. I know you're scared. I am too, and I don't even know who it is that's trying to hurt me, but I'd rather die than not be there when she takes her last breath. Please, Zane. Please do this for me. I won't fight you anymore. I won't try to escape, just, please... Please, give me this last moment with her."

Zane looks like a statue, his entire body is rigid, every muscle clenched. Terror is all I see when I look at him. A man terrified of what may happen. If he lets me go, and if he doesn't.

Like lightning striking, he snaps out of it. "We will go, but you will remain by my side the entire time. You will not go anywhere without me. If anything happens, we will leave and come back here. I will not risk your life. If it's not safe, we won't go inside."

He's barely finished laying down the ground rules, and I'm off the bed, running into the closet to get some clothes. I'm dressed in seconds and walk back out into the bedroom to find Zane standing in the same spot. He looks to be lost in thought, and my heart sinks into my stomach. Has he changed his mind?

When he sees me, his gaze flicks over my dressed form. "Ready to go?"

"Yes, are you?"

Crossing the space separating us, he takes my cheeks into his hands and leans down, so his lips are a centimeter away from my own. "I'm ready, but I've never been more scared of something happening to you than I am right now."

"Nothing will happen," I assure him even though I don't know anything about who is after us, or why they would want to hurt us.

"You're so naive and so good. I wouldn't expect you to understand how dangerous this is. I just want you to know that if something happens to you, anything at all, I will blame myself forever, and I'll gladly put a bullet between my own eyes. You're my world, and if you're not in it, then there is nothing left for me to live for."

I feel each word slicing through my skin and piercing my heart. This man is consuming me, and while I know I shouldn't feel a single thing for him, my emotions are twisting, becoming more confusing with each day I'm here. I shouldn't want Zane, but a part of me is drawn to him, to his darkness.

"Everything is going to be okay," I say before gently pressing my lips to his. I don't know what is going to happen. What I do know is that I have to get to Donna before it's too late.

∽

THE SUNLIGHT FEELS good against my skin after not seeing it for a while. I won't lie, I hate the reason we are leaving, but I'm happy to get some fresh air and leave the confines of that place. As it turns out, we are in the middle of nowhere, miles from the city, so even if I had escaped, it wouldn't have mattered much. The entire drive Zane white knuckles the steering wheel, his eyes darting between the rearview mirror and the windshield like someone is going to appear there.

I'm tempted to force him to tell me who is after us, and what all is going on, but I need to focus on the most important thing right now.

Donna had a stroke, the one and only person to ever care for me is most likely dying, and there isn't shit I can do about it.

Guilt clings to me as we get closer to the city. Maybe I should've spent more time with her, maybe I should've tried to get her into an even better nursing home, maybe something closer. The thoughts swirl like water running down a drain.

"Everything is going to be okay. I will always protect you... love you," Zane says, breaking the silence. It's like he knows how much I need someone to lean on.

Like he can feel the despair pumping through my veins. His words don't change what's happening right now though, and they don't make the loss of Donna any easier, but they do make me feel less alone.

"My heart hurts. It feels like I'm losing a piece of my soul." I swallow around the lump of emotions in my throat. "Donna was the only person to ever care for me. She adopted me when all hope was lost. When I was sure, I would forever be stuck in the system. Someone as sweet and caring as she doesn't deserve to die, especially from a stroke." I don't know why I'm telling him this, it's not like he doesn't already know everything about Donna and me.

Zane's hand comes to rest on my thigh, his touch makes my insides tingle.

"Donna doesn't deserve this, no, but we don't get to choose how someone dies."

I turn to him. "Says the one who kills people."

He gives me a sly grin, and my entire body warms all over. "Touché."

We arrive at the hospital a few minutes later, pulling into the emergency room parking lot. Zane parks, but before I can get out, he shakes his head, ordering me to stay put for a second. We're so close, and all I want to do is go inside and see Donna. Walking around the car, he opens my door and helps me out. His fingers interlock with mine as we walk across the sidewalk and into the hospital. With each step I take, the sicker I feel. Part of me wants to scream and yell and ask why the hell this is happening, and the other part just wants to break down and cry.

I remember Zane's instructions as we reach the round circular desk, where the receptionist is. *Don't talk to anyone. Keep your eyes down. Don't draw attention.* Staring down at our joined hands like they're the most majestic thing I've ever seen, I let Zane do all the talking while pretending like I'm not interested in the conversation.

"She's in the ICU. I'll send you down there, and one of the nurses will meet with you," the receptionist says. I don't even bother commenting on the fact that she's checking Zane out, drool basically dribbling down her chin. Jealousy has no place in my heart right now.

"Thank you," Zane says with a smile, and we head in the direction of the ICU, following the signs in the hospital.

When we reach the unit, there is a set of double doors that you have to be buzzed to get into. Zane squeezes my hand tighter and turns to me.

"It's going to be hard to see her like this. Are you sure this is what you want?"

"We're here, and we're going in. I don't care what condition she's in. I need to see her." My voice cracks, and my heart splinters in my chest. Zane nods and presses the button for us to be buzzed in. A second later, the door opens, and we walk into the ICU unit. There are monitors everywhere and things that sound like alarms going off.

Zane guides us up to yet another desk, where a woman in scrubs greets us.

"Hi, we've come to see Donna Miller."

The nurse walks around the desk and comes over to us, a folder in her hand. "Come with me, and we will discuss her condition."

I can hardly breathe, and suddenly I feel dizzy. Latching onto Zane's arm, I let him guide us where we need to go. "Donna is in critical condition right now. She's on a ventilator, and her brain function is..." The nurse pauses and frowns when she sees my reaction. I'm pretty sure I look like I'm about to pass out.

"She doesn't have any brain function?" I ask, my voice breaking at the end.

"This is very common after a stroke. Her brain was without oxygen for too long. The doctors have been looking for any brain activity, any signs that she'll recover, but as of this morning, there was nothing. I'm so sorry. The doctors have done all they can at this point. I can let you see her."

The tears I was holding back break free, and I swallow down a sob as I bury my face into Zane's side. He releases my hand and wraps his arms around me, holding me a little tighter. She's gone. The one and only person I ever had is gone. Physically, she's still here, but in the sense of her really being here, her spirit, she's gone.

The nurse takes us to her room, and what I see when I step inside has the ground crumbling beneath my feet. My knees go weak, and I feel like I'm going to pass out.

Donna. My sweet mom has tubes going in and out of her body everywhere. Her body is so still she doesn't even look alive, and in a way, I guess she isn't.

"I'll leave you alone for a bit," the nurse says, dismissing herself. The room spins around me, and I press a hand to my forehead to steady myself.

"Are you okay?" Zane's gravelly voice fills my ears. He turns me to face him, his hands circle my arms, holding me in place and blocking my view of Donna.

"She's just..." A sob escapes my lips, and I press my face into his shirt, gripping onto the fabric. It's like I'm losing everything.

"It's okay. I told you this was going to be hard, and it is. But you should be allowed to say goodbye. She would want that." I nod, blubbering into his shirt. I'm a mess, a complete mess. How will I survive this?

"I'm okay. I need to do this." I speak out loud, even though the words are just for me. Zane nods and takes a step back, releasing me, though it seems it's the last thing he wants to do. With him out of the way, I stand there for a long time, just staring at her. The woman who supported me when I felt hopeless. She nurtured and watered me, turned a wilted rose into a woman. I was lost before her and found the instant we met. Now she's leaving me again, and it feels like all those times I was left behind. Never the child picked. Forever alone.

Forcing my feet to move, I walk over to the side of the bed. I take her hand in mine. It's cold and makes me shiver at the touch. Of course, she doesn't react to my touch. She doesn't squeeze my hand. Doesn't even acknowledge that I'm there. The machines she's hooked up to make her chest rise and fall.

Seeing her like this breaks my heart. I miss seeing the smile on her face and the twinkle of joy in her eyes every time I would come and visit her. Never did I think the last time I saw her awake and happy would actually be the final time I'd see her that way. I can't stop the tears from falling as I stand there holding her hand. My shoulders drop, and I bite my lip to hold back a sob.

"I miss you already, and you aren't even gone yet." I wipe my face with the back of my hand. "I'm sorry I wasn't there; that I've been so busy and haven't been able to come and visit as much. I wish we had more time. That this didn't happen."

Sniffling, I continue. "I'm so thankful that you took me in and gave me a future. I've enjoyed every minute of being with you, and I am proud to call you my mom."

Bending down, I brush the grey hairs from her forehead and press a gentle kiss there. When I pull away, I'm crying so hard I can barely see. It's like I'm losing a piece of my soul, a piece of my upbringing.

"I've got you," Zane whispers, his arms circling my waist. He pulls me back against her chest, and I turn in his arms, needing someone to hold onto.

22

Zane

We stay for another twenty minutes, and I hate every second of it. I hate seeing Dove hurt, and I hate that we are here, out in the open where I can't protect her. Not the way I want to, at least. After a short while, I know I have to tell her it's time.

"Dove, we need to go. It's not safe to stay here."

She pulls away from my chest and nods in understanding. With her head hung low, I watch her walk over to Donna's side once more.

She says her tearful goodbyes before turning back to me. I hold my arms open, and she falls into them, letting me lead her outside the room. Donna will be given a proper funeral, it's the least I can do, and I know it will set Dove at ease to have her funeral taken care of.

"Everything is going to be okay, Dove. I promise it won't always hurt this bad." I try to console her, but her sobbing only intensifies. I walk her past the nurses' station and down the hall. I'm so focused on

Dove that I don't pay attention to our surroundings the way I should. All I can think about is getting us out of this hospital and back to the bunker.

We take the stairs down to the parking garage, and as soon as we step outside, something feels off. I pause, pulling Dove even closer.

"What's wrong?" she asks, peeking up at me through thick lashes.

"I don't know yet." I scan the area and spot two blacked-out SUVs in the same aisle we are parked. I take a step back, shoving Dove behind me as two car doors pop open. *Shit.*

Turning around, I take Dove's face into my hands and stare deeply into her eyes. "Listen to me. I need you to go back inside and find a place to hide. Hide until I come and find you, okay?" I try not to sound panicked, but this is my worst nightmare being brought to life.

"What's wrong?" She repeats, sounding more frantic this time. Tugging from my grasp, she tries to look over my shoulder.

"I'll explain everything to you later, please, just go and hide. Please, Dove," I say, feeling more desperate than I ever have before. She nods, and I release her, watching her step away from me. It hurts me physically to let her go, but I know I can't protect her if she's standing there watching me. I'm outnumbered and outgunned. I can't fight them and keep her safe at the same time. When she disappears through the door leading into the stairwell, I turn around to face whoever Christian has sent to get me.

Color me fucking shocked when I see the asshole himself walking toward me, a triumphant smile on his smug-ass weathered face. "Did you really think you could hide forever?"

I shrug. "I wasn't hiding from you. I was just taking a much-needed vacation." Maybe I can get him to talk a little bit, which will give Dove a little more time to hide.

"Do I look like a fucking idiot, Zane?" He cocks his head to the side. Each step he takes brings him closer and me closer to death.

Two men flank him, and I know he's got more men here somewhere. Christian is not stupid; he knows I could take out two guys with ease. As if they could read my mind, more car doors open, and four more men start to approach.

"Brought a lot of people just to chat," I say, forcing a grin on my lips.

"You know there is not going to be a whole lot of talking. Less talking, more killing."

"You brought a lot of people for that too. Did you forget how to hold a gun yourself?" I know provoking him is probably not my best bet right now, but fuck, I'm mad. Mad at him, mad at myself, mad at the world.

"Why shoot the gun myself when I have people that can do it for me? People like you. It's really a shame, you were one of my favorites. I guess it was my own fault for not finding the truth out sooner." He shakes his head like he still can't believe it.

"Find out what?"

"Find Dove... then find out who she is to you—"

I cut him off before he can finish. I don't want to hear him talk about my relationship with her, but I do want to know why the hell he wants her. "Why have you been looking for her for the last ten years?"

He chuckles. "So it was you who killed Billy. I knew I shouldn't have trusted that prick. Did you at least make him suffer first?"

"Am I known for delivering peaceful deaths?"

He laughs louder. "No. And that's exactly why it's going to hurt me to see you go. You could have had a long and prosperous career with me."

"Answer my question!" I growl. Two of his goons take a threatening step toward me, but Christian raises his hand, motioning for them to stay put. "Why do you want her?"

"Well, let's just say it's Castro's fault that I want her dead. But I don't want to bother you with the boring details since you are going to be busy dying. Rest assured, I'll take good care of your little Dove. I'll make sure my men have some fun with her before I kill her."

I lunge for him before his last words have left his mouth. I'm fast, but his men anticipated my move. Two of them are on me before I can even get close to Christian. I let my fist fly, hitting one of them right in the nose, bones crunching beneath my knuckles. The other one grabs my arm and twists it back painfully.

Twisting my body, I free myself and punch him in the chest in one move. The guy stumbles back but not before slugging me in the side of the head. My head is pounding, but I shake it off and try to push past him to get to Christian. When I look up, I freeze.

Christian is only a few feet away from me, his gun pointed at my chest. I hear the gun go off and I feel the hot searing pain lancing across my chest like fire moving outward. My body jerks back involuntarily as the bullet slices through my muscle and tissue.

"I guess for you, I can make an exception and pull the trigger myself, old friend," Christian says, and if I didn't know him any better, I would say he is actually a little bit remorseful for killing me. "Get the girl and bring her to me," he orders his men without looking away from me.

Anger and despair fill every fiber of my body. I want to kill him, want to kill every single one of his men, but all my body does is sag to the ground. I try to reach for my gun, but my limbs are useless. *I'm useless.* Dove is going to die. I'm going to lose everything.

"Goodbye, Zane..." Christian's voice sounds far away, but that can't be right. He was just here. I feel my eyes close, my mind fading away. No, no, no! I need to stay awake. I need to get to Dove, protect her.

I try to get up, but my body feels like it's made out of lead. My mind is whirling, and all I can think of is how much I hate Christian. How much I want to kill him right now. I used to think he was my savior, Dove's as well. He saved us both, and now he ends us both.

The memory of how it all began comes rushing forward. The beginning of the end.

"I'm not supposed to be released; you're making a mistake."

"I can't believe you're complaining about being released early. Be glad you get to leave. Mistake or not. You're no longer my problem," the prison guard says and shows me through the door.

I'm only seventeen, but for the last few months, I've done nothing but work out every day. Now I'm bigger than most kids my age, maybe that's why they deemed me mature enough for prison. I'd only spent a few weeks in juvenile detention before they shipped me off to the state penitentiary.

"Put this on." He throws a bag in front of my feet, and I quickly realize it's the clothes I wore the day they brought me in. I change out of my inmate uniform and into my old worn jeans and T-shirt.

Then it hits me. I'm about to walk out of here. Free. But I have nowhere to go. I hate to admit it, even to myself, but here I know what was coming every morning. Every day was the same, an endless cycle of structure and routines. On the outside, there is nothing but chaos.

I'll be lost.

Twenty minutes later, I'm outside, standing in a parking lot with nothing but two twenty-dollar bills in my hand. What the fuck am I supposed to do now?

I start walking down the sidewalk, not knowing what else to do. I can't just stand there. I make it about half a mile down the road when a blacked-out SUV pulls up to me. The window is being rolled down, and some guy appears on the other side.

"I don't need a ride," I bark out before he can say a word.

"You must be Zane," the guy I've never seen before says.

"How the fuck do you know my name?" I stop walking, and the car stops moving at the same time.

"I'm Christian, and I'm the one who got you released early."

"And why would you do that?" I ask suspiciously.

"Why don't you get in and we can talk about it."

"I'm not getting into that car with you to suck your cock. Go ask what happened to the last guy who tried that shit. Oh, wait, you can't, 'cause I fucking killed his ass."

The guy named Christian throws back his head and starts laughing out loud. He laughs for ten minutes straight before he can compose himself enough to talk again.

"I like you already, Zane. Don't worry, I'm not into that either. I want you to work for me... taking care of people. Just like you took care of that guy you were talking about."

"What's in it for me?"

"Anything you want. Money, power, women, drugs. Name it, and it's yours."

Maybe I should have just kept walking that day. Maybe I could have kept her safe in a different way. I guess I'll never find out. The past is the past, and there is nothing I can do to change any of that now. My eyes fall shut, and this time, I can't pry them back open. I fade in and out of consciousness, knowing deep down, that this is it. I'm going to die.

Pictures of everything I've ever loved in my life flash before my eyes, every single one an image of Dove.

23

Dove

Forcing air into my lungs, I focus on each step I take. The last thing I want to do is trip and fall or injure myself. I'm not sure who is after us, but I don't want to find out. The fear in Zane's eyes was enough for me to stop asking questions and just listen.

I should be jumping for joy right now, planning my escape, but I can't even consider that knowing that Zane is back there going through god knows what. Yes, I know I should feel different, but I can't. I just can't. My stomach churns when I think about something bad happening to him. *Shit*, I think I'm going to be sick. Gripping onto the metal railing, I stop on the stairs and gulp precious oxygen into my lungs.

It feels like an elephant is sitting on my chest. Like no matter how much air I breathe in, I'm never really catching my breath. A door opens a flight above me, and I force my feet to move, carrying me down the stairs. I don't make it but a few feet before I hear someone descending the steps. *No.* Not someone, there are two sets of footsteps. Two people.

"You can run, but you can't hide..." That voice is like nails on a chalkboard, and fear trickles down my spine at the sound. Immediately, I start running down the steps. I need to get out of this stairwell. It's like a trap. If I stay here, I'm as good as caught. Dead.

When I get to the bottom floor, I grab the door handle and twist it open. Cold air whips through my hair as I make it outside. The door falls shut behind me and I get ready to start running down the street when I stop dead in my tracks. Two men standing a mere ten feet away, smiles that promise horrible things on their faces.

What do I do? Where do I go?

Like a trapped mouse, I look for a way out, but there isn't one. I can't go back into the stairwell. I can't go forward either.

"Give it up, baby, just come with us, and maybe we'll take it easy on you... maybe we won't kill you right away. We can always have a little fun, give you a little pleasure..."

My eyes dart around the space, there is nowhere to go. I'm trapped. Zane told me to run, to hide. I can't die like this. I won't die like this.

"Don't even think about it." If his voice didn't scare me half to death, the scar running from eye to chin on his face would.

What do I do? I feel the panic rising, bubbling over inside of me. The hairs on the back of my neck stand on end. This is bad. Something terrible is going to happen. Zane was right. He was right. The next moment, the door behind me opens and the before I can turn around a hand slams over my lips while an arm wraps around my middle.

Releasing a blood-curdling scream, I struggle with all my might, kicking my legs and flailing in his grasp. One kick must hit its mark because a second later, the guy releases me, a harsh *fuck* filling my ears. I don't think I just start running. I make it all of ten feet before I'm cut off. My lungs burn, and my muscles are tense, fear and panic overtake my body. It's fight or die, and I can't die yet.

"We told you we'd take it easy on you if you were a good girl, but of course, you couldn't come quietly... looks like we have to do things the hard way." One of the men pulls out a gun, and I open my mouth to scream, but the sound never comes. Before I can react, he's on me, the butt of his gun flashes over my vision before it connects with the side of my head. Crumpling to the ground, the entire world goes dark around me.

~

WHEN I COME TO, my entire body is throbbing, and my head feels like someone ran it over with a bus. Blinking my eyes open, I resist the urge to cringe at the bright light dangling above my head. *What the—* I don't finish the thought as I realize by looking down at my hands that I'm tied to a chair, my wrists bound to the arms. Flickering through my memories, I try and recollect how I got here.

Donna. Hospital. Zane. Knocked out.

"Help! Someone help!" I call out to anyone who might hear me while pulling against the ropes that bind me to the chair. I need to find Zane, need to get out of here and away from these people. A soft chuckle fills the room, and I whip my head around, looking for the person the voice belongs to, but I don't see anyone. Darkness surrounds me, except for the tiny light hanging above my head. I try and swallow down my fear, but it's suffocating me.

"Well, hello, Dove." A man appears before me, he looks like a mobster, in a nice suit. His beady eyes trail over my body, and I can feel every single movement. "It's a pleasure to finally meet you, granted it's not under the best circumstances." He motions to the rope and chair. "I'm sorry, I couldn't offer you better accommodations. I'm Christian," he says his name like I should know it.

"Where is Zane? Where am I? Why did you take me?" The questions pour out of me like an overflowing sink. I doubt this man will give me an answer, but I still ask. I have to.

"Zane?" He leans into my face, and I crane my head back to put some distance between us. The man's voice smells of liquor, and that only intensifies my fear. Tremors wrack my body, and I start to shake as if I'm cold. "Zane is dead. I left his body back in the parking garage." He pauses as if to take in my facial expression. Then his lips curl up into a tiny smirk as he watches me take in what he just told me.

Zane is dead. My chest tightens, and my heart hurts. I feel like a piece of my soul shatters. Rationally, I shouldn't care if he's dead, but for some reason, I feel connected to him. Like I've known him my entire life.

"I mean, it really is such a shame that he dies after all this time. It took you so many years to find each other again just for him to leave you..." Christian frowns, and then without warning, he reaches out and grabs me by the back of the neck, his fingers digging into the tender flesh hard enough to leave bruises.

"I... I don't... understand. What are you talking about?" Confusion swirls. "I don't know Zane. He kidnapped me, and..." The words keep coming until Christian squeezes the back of my neck so hard the words cut off, and pain consumes me.

"Don't lie to me, you little bitch. I know all about your connection to Zane. It took me long enough, but I finally figured it out."

He pulls back my head and stares directly into my eyes. He must see my genuine confusion because a moment later, he lets out a humorless laugh I feel in my bones.

"You really don't know, do you? Does the name William ring a bell?"

Now I'm even more confused. How does he know about William, and what does he have to do with anything? The information isn't adding up in my brain, or maybe I just don't care to try and add it together.

"William... he's dead. I saw him die... I was there."

"He didn't die, sweetheart. He recovered, and a few months later, he went back and killed your foster dad in cold blood. William Zane Brennen was a born killer, and that's exactly why I hired him."

Like an atomic bomb, everything around me explodes.

Zane is William.

William is Zane.

Christian shakes me by my neck, dragging me out of my own mind.

"Let me tell you the rest of the story, Dove. When I found him in prison, he was killing guys left and right, even though he was one of the youngest inmates. I found a way to get him out so he could work for me. His talent was really wasted in prison. He did well for himself too. Worked his way up, became one of my best men. Little did I know, he had been hiding the one thing I'd been looking for all along. You."

Me? What does he want with me? I can't fully wrap my head around it. Not around any of this. I have so many questions, so many, but I guess it's too late for any answer now. Zane... William is gone.

When the asshole let's go of my neck, I lull to the side, staring off into nothingness. How couldn't I see it? How did I not put one and one together? Why didn't he tell me?

Now he's gone, and I... I'm going to die. He warned me, and I didn't listen. Tears swim in my eyes.

"You know I sent him to kill you?" His menacing voice draws me back to the present, and I shiver at the darkness of it. "He took you into hiding instead. I guess I should thank him for that. Killing you would have been a waste of something good, I see that now." His eyes roam down my body, and I feel vomit rising in my throat.

"What... What is going to happen to me?" It's a stupid question to ask when you're obviously standing on the edge of death, but I have to know if that's where I'm going. If I'm going to die right now. "Are you still going to kill me?"

Christian smiles, and I feel the promise of pain in that one single look. "I was going to, but it's your lucky day because I'm feeling generous, and well, I have a much better use for you now." Before I can respond, his fist comes out of nowhere, his knuckles crashing into the side of my face. Pain lances across my face, and all I can think before everything goes black is that I should've listened to Zane.

∼

Thank you for reading Cruel Obsession!!! Up next is Deadly Obsession, which is the second and final book in this series!

ALSO BY THE AUTHORS

CONTEMPORAY ROMANCE

North Woods University
The Bet
The Dare
The Secret
The Vow
The Promise
The Jock

Bayshore Rivals
When Rivals Fall
When Rivals Lose
When Rivals Love

Breaking the Rules
Kissing & Telling

Also by the Authors

Babies & Promises
Roommates & Thieves

***

DARK ROMANCE

The Blackthorn Elite
Hating You
Breaking You
Hurting You
Regretting You

The Obsession Duet
Cruel Obsession
Deadly Obsession

The Rossi Crime Family
Protect Me
Keep Me
Guard Me
Tame Me
Remember Me

The Moretti Crime Family
Savage Beginnings
Violent Beginnings
Broken Beginnings

The King Crime Family

Indebted
Inevitable

The Diabolo Crime Family
Devil You Hate
Devil You Know

Corium University

King of Corium
Drop Dead Queen
Broken Kingdom

***

STANDALONES

Convict Me

Runaway Bride

His Gift

Two Strangers

This Christmas

Beck and Hallman

www.bleedingheartromance.com

beck.hallman@gmail.com

facebook @beckandhallman

Printed in Great Britain
by Amazon